NEW YORK

JAMIE LEE GREY

Cover design by Deranged Doctor Design.

www.derangeddoctordesign.com

Created with Vellum

To the remnant in America.
Though you be few,
May you be faithful.

CONTENTS

CHAPTER ONE

Incessant pounding rattled her consciousness. Katie Nelson forced her eyes open. Where was she? She blinked and looked around.

The motorhome. Right. Camping this week.

The pounding continued.

Wait! She sat straight up in bed, banging her head on the top of the cabover sleeping area. The fires! They'd fled California. Where were they now?

"Katie!" A woman's voice called during a pause in the pounding.

What? Who? She crawled over Zach and climbed down the ladder. Timothy was beginning to stir from his sleep, and Duke had planted himself in front of the door. Hackles up.

A low growl emanated from his throat.

Zach rolled over and mumbled something incoherent.

The pounding resumed.

"Hold on! I'm coming!" Katie fumbled with the lock. The motorhome door's window was etched, so she couldn't see who was outside, but whoever it was knew her name.

Knew her.

"Hush!" She commanded the black Great Dane, pushing him out of her way with her hip. She swung the door open.

Morning had arrived, with bright sun, gusty wind, and her fellow traveler from last night. Jennifer looked almost as worried as she had the previous evening, approaching the wall of flames. In leather sandals and a yellow summer dress, she stood in the hotel's rear parking lot, looking over her shoulder as if expecting someone to come out after her.

"Are you okay?" Katie asked. Rather than invite her into the RV with her giant dog and sleeping husband and child, she stepped out and closed the door.

Jennifer twisted her hands together and focused huge hazel eyes on Katie. The breeze lifted strands of her short brown hair.

"You're on TV!" She blurted.

Katie blinked, then frowned. "What? Me?"

"Your husband, actually," Jennifer looked at the motorhome door as if expecting Zach to make an appearance.

"Why?"

"Oh, dear. Oh, dear!" She clasped her hands in front of her chest and looked at the pavement. "I probably shouldn't have said anything."

"What?" This didn't sound good. The woman had stormed out here, woke them up, and now changed her mind about sharing her news? "What's going on? Why is he on TV?"

Jennifer raised watery eyes to meet Katie's stare. Her chin trembled.

"They say he's a person of interest."

"What are you talking about? Person of interest in what?"

Glancing over her shoulder again, Jennifer took a step back. "I shouldn't have come."

Katie grabbed her arm. "Jennifer! Look at me!"

As the woman glanced back toward her, Katie released her arm.

"Please! Tell me what's going on!"

Jennifer began to cry, burbling sobs. "I might get in trouble!"

She turned suddenly and started back toward the hotel. Katie raced around her in her bare feet, then planted herself in front of the woman. She grabbed both of her arms this time, and stared into her weepy eyes.

"Jennifer! We saved your life last night! You have to tell me what is going on."

The lady swallowed, looked around Katie toward the hotel, then looked back toward the motorhome. Finally, her eyes turned to Katie's.

"The fires," she whispered. "They say he's a person of interest in the fires!"

Katie's hands fell from Jennifer's arms as her jaw fell open. What? That was the craziest thing she'd ever heard!

Suddenly free, Jennifer bolted toward the hotel. Katie watched her go, and knew she should run after her, but she was stunned into immobility.

Frozen in shock. Her husband? A suspect? Ridiculous!

But Jennifer, whom they'd rescued out of the path of the fires last night, was so ambivalent about even telling her. What if she was going back to call the cops?

"WAIT!" Katie sprang into motion, chasing Jennifer across the parking lot. Bits of gravel and debris chewed at her bare feet as she ran.

The older woman was no match for her, and Katie overtook her before Jennifer was halfway back to the building.

"Wait!" Katie grabbed her arm again, slowing her movement. "Stop, Jennifer!"

The woman slowed, then stopped. Her expression had changed from worry to fear. Fear? Of Katie? Who'd saved her life?

"Jennifer," she huffed out between quick breaths. "Please. We helped you. We aren't terrorists. Think!"

"How do I know?" She turned round eyes on Katie. "You might've – I don't know – but he's on television!"

She pointed back to the RV, where Zach was just stepping out, blond hair ruffled by the breeze, still in the shorts and t-shirt he'd worn to bed. Similar to the attire Katie was in at the moment.

"Jennifer, he's a blogger and a worship pastor at a church! We were doing volunteer work this weekend! Not lighting fires. Come on!"

The woman still looked skeptical.

"He was the one who stopped to help you, when nobody else would," Katie persisted. "You think he's a terrorist?"

Jennifer kept her eyes on him. "Maybe not."

"Think, Jennifer! We have a four year old child. A dog. I'm a journalist. We're normal people in an old RV, not – not – terrorists!"

Katie couldn't believe she was having this conversation. Maybe she wasn't. Maybe she was having a nightmare, and she'd wake up in a few minutes.

Yeah. That must be it. A nightmare. Thank God!

A knock sounded at the front door, and Evan Nelson set the last dish in the drain rack and dried his hands on a dishtowel.

"I'll get it!"

Hopefully his parents, in the rear of the house, heard him. He strode through the living room and glanced through the small window. It was the gentleman who owned a summer cabin just down the road from theirs. Evan opened the door. The man smiled, his blue eyes twinkling.

"Hello, Evan. I'm not sure if you remember me –"

"Of course I do, Ambassador Wilford." Evan stepped back, pulling the door fully open. "Won't you come in?"

"Thank you, but no, I can't." The thin, grey-haired man glanced back toward the road. "My daughter has a flat tire, and I would change it, but she doesn't seem to carry a jack in her vehicle!"

Evan remembered the ambassador's daughter. Growing up and spending summer vacations here in Galloway, one got to know all the children in the community, because there weren't very many. She was about four years younger than himself, a truly pesky taga-long. A twerp.

"No problem. I've got a jack." Evan joined the ambassador on the front porch. "Let me grab it from my pickup, and I'll give you a hand."

"That would be very nice. Thank you."

Evan retrieved the jack and a lug wrench, and walked down the short driveway to the main road. Elizabeth's blue Audi was parked at the edge of the gravel road. The driver's door opened, and she stepped out, wearing denim shorts and a white blouse.

"You remember my daughter, Elizabeth?" Ambassador Wilford asked.

Evan gulped. He remembered her, alright, but this was *not* what he remembered! This was a beautiful woman, with long legs and glossy auburn hair and huge green eyes. Not a twerp!

"Uh, yeah," he finally managed, setting down the tools and extending his hand. To his relief, she stepped forward and grasped it.

"Hi, Evan. It's been a long time." She smiled then, a knockout smile that lit her face and eyes like sunshine.

He could barely breathe. He swallowed. Reminded himself to stop staring.

"Yeah," he said. He couldn't think of anything to say. Where were his words? What happened to his language skills? Cat got his tongue?

Embarrassed, he bent down and picked up his lug wrench. At least he still knew how to change a tire. Sheesh!

He loosened the lug nuts slightly, then jacked up the vehicle, removed the lug nuts, put on her spare tire, partially tightened the lug nuts, lowered the Audi, and finished tightening the nuts. He didn't say a word the entire time, but he was constantly aware of her mesmerizing presence. Her little black sandals and slim calves stayed in his peripheral vision as he worked.

Finally, he stood up.

"Well. I think you're good to go." He looked at her lovely face, with high cheekbones, red lips and those eyes – those amazing green eyes!

"Thank you," Elizabeth said. She looked toward her dad. "Ready?"

"Yes." The ambassador turned his gaze on Evan. "But why don't you join us for lunch, Evan. Around noon?"

Elizabeth glanced his way. Waiting for an answer.

"Uh, yeah. Yep. That would be great!" He nodded and smiled. The pair got into the Audi. Evan picked up his tools.

He was such a dope! He'd lost his entire grasp of the English language for the better part of ten minutes! He sounded like a hayseed, not like the college professor he'd finally become. Ugh.

Head low, he trudged up the driveway. Elizabeth must think he was an idiot.

How'd she become so beautiful? She'd been a scrawny kid, annoying him and his big brother Zach every time they turned around. She followed them around, trying to climb the trees they climbed, splashing the water when they looked for frogs in Simpson Creek, all that annoying kid stuff.

And now, she looked like a model. He should've been nicer to her!

He put the tools back in his pickup. Perhaps he'd have a chance to redeem himself at lunch. Noon wasn't that far off.

Which meant it was almost 9 a.m. on the west coast. Maybe he could reach Zach and Katie now.

He pulled out his cell phone and dialed.

And got the newly familiar, "All circuits are busy. Please try your call again later" message. He sighed. Hopefully they were okay. The last time he'd talked to them was yesterday, when they'd been on their way out of California.

Zach had called to ask him to get Mom and Dad, and leave Baltimore for the remainder of the weekend.

So here they were, on this lovely Sunday morning, in Galloway, West Virginia. At their summer cabin in the Allegheny Mountains. Just down the road from the ambassador to Israel, Hank Wilford, and his suddenly stunning daughter.

Elizabeth.

A strong rap sounded on her door. Vice President Alana Mills yawned as she walked across the plush ivory carpet and opened it. In the hallway, a steward in military uniform held a silver breakfast tray. She moved aside so he could enter her cramped temporary quarters.

"Just set it on the little table there."

He moved efficiently into her room, set the tray on the table and returned to the doorway.

"Can I get you anything else?"

"No. Thank you." She had a fleeting thought about tipping him, which was a ridiculous vestige of her days in private life.

The steward turned to go, and Alana nodded at the Secret Service agent who guarded her door. This layer of security seemed silly, given that they were currently in a bunker under the East Wing of the White House. Designed to withstand a nuclear attack, the Presidential Emergency Operations Center was about as secure as anywhere in the world. And she was resting in a wing off of it. What'd she need Secret Service for down here?

Protection from the breakfast steward?

Whatever.

She closed her door, turned to the tray and whisked off the shiny cover. Black tea steamed from a delicate teacup. A veggie omelet with a side of gourmet potatoes made her mouth water. Sitting down, she lifted the fork and dug in. Hadn't realized how hungry she was... after eating so little yesterday, then being up all night working, she was famished.

And tired. She glanced at the clock. Almost noon!

She'd managed several hours of sleep after presenting her team's ideas to the president this morning.

Basilia Hernandez had swiftly chosen the one originally suggested by Governor Abdullah – may he rest in peace. It'd seemed inevitable that he would have died in the California fires last night, given the situation at the time of his final phone call to the president.

It was so ironic that he'd been killed in the terrorist attack that his own son had instigated. Weird karma? And what about his son? Had he lived or died? The last she'd heard of Nadir, he was on foot, running from the fires.

It didn't really matter now. If he was dead, good. If he was alive, he'd never be prosecuted for his crimes. They'd already selected a fall guy to blame for burning down the state: Zachary James Nelson, a big-time religious and political blogger who'd organized a cadre of church volunteers for California's annual Coastal Cleanup Day.

Nelson, also a worship pastor, was the perfect patsy, actually – he'd placed hundreds of people all along the coast on the morning the coastal fires started. With a little manipulation of the facts, it was easy to pin it on him. Governor Abdullah was a genius, even if his only motive was to protect the Muslim community and preserve his own legacy. And to destroy a political enemy, of course.

Alana wolfed another bite of the exquisite omelet. One of the best things about living in the upper echelon of society was the constant availability of world-class food. She had to be careful not to get fat.

As she chewed, her thoughts focused on the hunt for the fall guy. Had he been arrested yet? How in the world were they going to make the charges stick to him? They'd contrived a good bit of circumstantial evidence, sure – but any decent defense lawyer would inevitably get him off the hook for this.

Since he actually hadn't done it, after all.

Also, there was the irritating little problem of explaining how Mr. Nelson had set off the second – and far deadlier – line of fires yesterday afternoon. They'd either have to come up with something, or just say that part was still under investigation. Or that he'd sent his arsonists east to light the afternoon fires immediately after they'd lit the morning ones. That would work.

She sipped her tea. Too hot. And needed sugar!

Well, maybe they'd get lucky and he'd get assassinated or something, killed in jail or whatever, and they'd never have to go to trial. Then the country would forever blame him for burning down the state, and never look for the real culprits. Like Lee Harvey Oswald, if he hadn't really assassinated President John F. Kennedy. There would always be conspiracy theories, but Americans would generally believe what the media and government told them.

In fact, that was actually a great idea! Arrange Zachary Nelson's untimely death.

Suddenly, she was wide awake and couldn't wait to get back to the group assembled in the PEOC and whisper her idea in a few ears.

She downed the last bit of omelet, ignoring the fancy potatoes, and hurried into the minuscule bathroom. These bunker accommodations left a lot to be desired. Hopefully, she and her colleagues might be able to get out of here today, now that the crisis was past, and return to the more commodious environments to which they were all accustomed.

CHAPTER TWO

Katie swayed slightly. Her legs felt like posts. Like at any moment, the morning breeze would topple her over. She moistened her lips and focused on her fellow traveler.

"Look, Jennifer, just promise me this –"

Jennifer's wary eyes turned to meet hers.

"Promise me you won't do anything. Won't call the cops, won't say anything to anybody."

She didn't respond.

"Look, we didn't do it! We're innocent! But we need a few minutes to get dressed and – and...."

And what, exactly? What on earth were they going to do? Katie couldn't imagine giving Zach this news. She focused back on Jennifer.

"And I have to clear my head. I can't think straight right now. We have a little boy...." Katie's gaze turned back to the RV, where Zach was leading Duke out toward some bushes, while Timothy hurried after them, a little angel with sun-kissed blond hair.

Jennifer's face softened. Katie moved in to take advantage of that moment.

"I promise we had nothing to do with this, Jennifer. Nothing at all. I don't know how we got caught up in it, but I promise it will get sorted out and you'll see we're innocent."

Jennifer bit her lip. "Then why –"

"I have no idea! Honestly!" Katie suddenly felt lightheaded. She swayed again and reached out, steadying herself on Jennifer's shoulder. "I can't believe this is happening."

"What are you going to do? He needs to turn himself in," Jennifer said, pointing at Zach. "If he's innocent, it'll all get cleared up."

Would it? It should, but... Katie wasn't sure. She'd had some friends prosecuted once for something they absolutely hadn't done. It took two years and well over a hundred thousand dollars to clear their names.

Katie and Zach didn't have a hundred thousand dollars.

"I don't feel so good."

Darkness swirled the periphery of her vision. Her knees gave out and she found herself dropping toward the pavement. Jennifer caught her under her arms and eased her to a sitting position.

"Are you okay? Should I call an ambulance?"

"No!" Katie sucked in fresh air. "I just need a minute. I –"

"You need a doctor!" Jennifer looked like a mother now, hovering in front of Katie's face.

"No." Katie drew a deep breath and blew it out. "I can't believe this is happening."

She glanced back toward Zach, who was holding Duke's leash in one hand and Timothy's hand in the other. Such a good man! How could anyone ever accuse him of something like this?

What if Jennifer was wrong?

Could she have been mistaken?

Katie's gaze flew to her face.

"Jennifer, are you sure? Maybe the television showed someone who looks like Zach? Not actually him?"

She shook her head definitively. "No. It was him, I'm positive."

"Did they say his name?"

Jennifer pursed her lips. She cocked her head a little.

Maybe this was all a big misunderstanding! Even if Jennifer had it right, maybe Zach's photo was shown with another man's name, or maybe –

"They did." Jennifer nodded. "Or at least, I saw it on that little scroll screen that runs across the bottom of the news broadcasts."

"The chyron," Katie said.

"Sure. Whatever it's called."

Oh, Lord. What if this was real? What were they going to do? Katie knew she should pray, but all she could say was, "Oh, Lord."

More words would come later. More prayers. For now, she just needed to know He was there. Even now, in the midst of the most bizarre moment of her life.

Her vision cleared and her strength returned. She pushed off the pavement and stood up.

"Jennifer." When the woman's gaze met hers, she continued. "Please don't call the police or anybody. We need a little time to get our heads around this. Because we didn't do it!"

Jennifer glanced back at the hotel.

"They'll know I told you. There's security cameras, they would have seen me coming out here." Suddenly she shuddered. "I arrived here with you! What if they think I'm an accomplice?"

Katie's chest tightened. "Don't you see how crazy this is? You're not an accomplice, any more than we're terrorists!"

Jennifer didn't respond.

"We all need a little time to think," Katie implored. "Okay?"

Slowly, Jennifer nodded. "Yeah. Okay."

She took a step toward the hotel, then stopped and looked back. "Good luck, Katie."

Sudden tears muddled Katie's vision. She took a deep breath. "Thank you."

Jennifer walked toward the hotel, and Katie turned back

toward the Minnie Winnie. Zach was holding the motorhome's door open. Duke bounded in, followed by Timothy. Zach turned and looked at her. No doubt wondering what that was all about.

She'd have to tell him. They'd have to figure out what to do.

And quickly, before Jennifer ratted them out. Katie couldn't rely on her to keep her word. That woman was too ambivalent. She couldn't be trusted.

Evan Nelson pulled his other shirt from his duffel and put it on. It was a little nicer than the one he'd been wearing when the ambassador knocked on their door. He hadn't packed many clothes, since he'd only brought his parents out here for the weekend. They'd planned to return home this afternoon, but maybe they could stay another night.

He didn't have any classes scheduled until tomorrow afternoon. They could leave early in the morning and make it back in time. Or he could have his graduate assistant cover his Monday classes.

He combed his short brown hair and examined his beard. He'd only grown it because it made him look older and more professorial. Without it, he looked more like he was 19, instead of 26. He made a point of keeping it neatly trimmed, though.

Leaning toward the mirror, he double checked everything. Probably as good as it was going to get. He wasn't lucky enough to be born with Zach's blue eyes. He got plain brown ones.

Well, at least they worked. His vision was nearly 20/20.

He glanced at his cell phone. Ten till noon. Time to go!

Hustling down the creaky stairs, he found his parents in the kitchen. Dad was nearly as tall while sitting at the table as mom was while standing at the sink. She claimed to be five feet even, but Evan stopped believing that when he stopped believing in the

Easter Bunny. If she was four-foot-eleven, she was probably wearing wedge heels.

"Ambassador Wilford invited me to lunch," he announced. "Because I changed a flat tire for them this morning."

"Them?" His mom turned from the sink to study his face.

No doubt it was growing redder by the second. Good thing he had that beard!

"Uh, yeah. His daughter was with him."

"Liz," his dad said, glancing up from his newspaper. "She's a cutie."

"She goes by Elizabeth now." Evan grabbed his keys from the bowl on the countertop. "I'm gonna be late. See ya!"

He rushed out of there, sure his parents were exchanging knowing glances. It'd been a year since his long-time girlfriend had dumped him. And he hadn't dated anyone since. His family had been needling him about when he was going to find a nice girl and settle down.

He wanted to. He just had a hard time finding a nice girl. Most of the young women he knew were defensive. Easily and instantly "offended" by anything. Not to mention controlling, bossy or manipulative. Who wanted to spend the rest of their life with someone like that?

Launching down the front steps, he hurried to his pickup and jumped in. Turning the key, the engine roared to life, and he raced off to Elizabeth's house. Uh, the ambassador's vacation home. Whatever.

He turned in the driveway and pulled up in front of the log cabin, between Elizabeth's Audi and a black SUV with dark windows.

As he walked up the steps, the door opened.

Evan smiled as the ambassador stepped outside. He didn't look happy. His eyebrows drew together.

"Have you heard?" he asked.

Evan cocked his head. "Heard what?"

"The news! Have you been watching the news?"

"About the fires. Yeah, we watched last night."

"No." Ambassador Wilford shook his head slowly and held Evan's gaze. "About your brother."

"What? Zach?" He suddenly couldn't breathe. Had Zach died in the fires? Hadn't he and Katie been able to get out? What about their little boy, Timothy?

He reached for a beam supporting the porch roof, and steadied himself. "Is he okay? Was he killed?"

"You better come inside and sit down." The ambassador reached for his arm.

"My parents..." Evan looked back to his truck, then whirled to Mr. Wilford. "What happened to Zach?!"

Elizabeth appeared in the doorway.

"Evan." Her voice was smooth like honey. "Please come in."

She held the door open for him, and his feet followed her into the cozy cabin. It'd been a decade or more since he'd been there, but everything looked exactly as it had then, before her mother died.

"Please, sit down." Elizabeth pointed to the sofa.

"Tell me what happened!" He eased himself onto the couch, looking from her to her father.

The ambassador pursed his lips, exchanged a glance with his daughter, and finally settled into the chair across from him.

"I'm sorry, Evan. Your brother is wanted for questioning."

"Oh!" Relief flooded through him. "You had me scared there for a minute. I thought he'd died or something!"

They said nothing, but their expressions were grim. Evan moistened his lips.

"Questioning... about what?"

Elizabeth drew a noisy breath. "He's a person of interest. In the California fires."

Her words smashed into him like an iron fist.

When he regained his senses, he looked from one to the other.

"What? No...." Evan's eyes focused on the ambassador's. "No!"

He leapt to his feet. "That's crazy! He's a pastor, for crying out loud!"

Alana Mills took the fastest shower she'd ever had, toweled herself off, dressed in a dark blue skirt and jacket with a cream silk blouse, and wiped the fogged-up mirror. Just a bit of makeup would perk up her flawless brown skin, but her hair was going to take a little more time. It always did.

She half-dried it with the hair dryer, fingered styling cream through her jet-black curls, and called it good enough.

Who would really care how she looked in a bunker, anyway?

Jamming her feet into too-high heels, she grabbed her briefcase and headed out the door. Down the hall with its old-school crimson carpet, and right into the PEOC.

Her new world.

Everyone was there. Of course, most of them had headed to bed by 3 a.m., while she'd kept working five more hours.

The president looked up as she slid into her chair. She gave Alana a grin and a thumbs-up.

Oh, good! Alana smiled back. Things must be going their way. Finally.

She glanced at her chief of staff. Jason looked like he hadn't slept a wink. He'd worked almost as late as she had. Bags underlined his brown eyes, and his straight black hair was slightly disheveled. Like he'd ran out of the shower and forgotten to comb it. His red tie was askew, too.

He leaned toward her and whispered in her ear.

"We've put out a media alert on that blogging pastor who organized the churches for yesterday's Clean Up the Coast thing in California. Since he brought so many people to the locations near where the fires started, all along the entire coast, the media is sucking it up. They love it!"

Alana grinned. Of course they did!

Stooges.

"Has he been arrested yet?" Her eyes met his.

Jason shook his head. "No, but it's just a matter of time. You can run, but you can't hide from the all-seeing eyes of the United States government!"

She smiled. He was certainly right about that!

They'd catch this guy in short order. He wouldn't know what hit him!

CHAPTER THREE

Katie forced herself to move across the parking lot to where Zach waited outside the motorhome. She could barely walk straight, and certainly couldn't think straight.

"Is Jennifer okay?" Zach asked, his blond mop all bedhead.

Katie shook her head. "It's not her –"

She couldn't say the words. How could she tell her husband that he was the focus of a terrorist attack on the entire state of California?

It was shocking. Crazy. Absurd beyond belief.

Zach studied her with those deep blue eyes. "Are *you* okay?"

"No." She reached the steps and sat down. Took a deep breath. Looked back into those baby blues. Had to say the words. "She said...."

Her mind blanked. How could she tell him? How could this be happening to them?

"Spit it out, Katie."

She gulped. "She said you were on TV. That you're a person of interest."

His face was blank, like none of that registered. Finally, a twinge of comprehension flickered in his eyes.

"I was on TV?"

"They think you started the fires!"

He stared at her like she was totally nuts.

"I'm not making this up, Zach! She came out here to tell me!"

He just looked at her, not responding. She stood up.

"Baby, this is serious! What are we going to do?"

Still no response. Was he in a trance? Dumbfounded? In shock?

Slowly, so slowly, his eyes focused on hers. His head tilted slightly. His mouth opened, but no words came out.

"Zach," she pleaded. "Say something!"

He shook his head. Left. Right. Left. Right. Then he drew a long breath.

"What?" He stared at her. Definitely dumbfounded.

"We have to figure out what to do! You're a person of interest in the terrorist attack!" She grasped his hand. "They think you did it, Zach."

Tears welled into her eyes again. And spilled onto her cheeks.

"They think we're terrorists," she sobbed.

He jerked his hand away. "That's crazy, Kate!"

"I know." She gulped air. "I know!"

A long moment of silence passed between them.

"What are we gonna do?" she whispered.

He rubbed his forehead, then took a step back. His gaze flitted around, then landed on her. His lips parted, and he inhaled.

"I need to get dressed."

"Zach!" She tightened her fists. "What are we going to do?"

"I don't know!" He brushed past her and rushed up the steps into the RV.

Katie stood alone in the parking lot, in the shorts and tank top she'd slept in, looking toward the hotel. The breeze lifted her long brown hair, teasing it over her shoulders. Was Jennifer calling the cops right now? Or was she keeping her word?

One thing was for sure – Katie would never know. Not until it was too late, anyway.

Birds chirped in the trees planted in the green space at the edge of the parking lot. How could they sound so happy? Didn't they know the world had just come crashing down?

First, on the entire state of California.

And now, on the Nelson family, who'd barely escaped with their lives.

She rubbed her arms. Far in the distance, beyond the hotel parking lot and the highway and the chirping birds, she heard another sound, and it made her blood run cold.

A siren.

Evan sank back onto the ambassador's couch. Elizabeth disappeared into the kitchen, and he heard water running.

His hands pressed against his temples as his eyes mis-focused on the pattern in the blue carpet.

Was this for real? What should he do? His dad would have a heart attack if Evan gave him this news.

He choked, then coughed.

Elizabeth's soft footsteps approached, and he looked up to see her holding out a glass of ice water. Mechanically, his hand reached up and accepted it.

"Thank you." It didn't sound like his voice. Weirdly younger, and lost. He swallowed some water, then cleared his throat.

The ambassador sat quietly in the crimson chair across from him, watching his every move. Evan tried to figure out what to say.

"I –" He started over. "This – this is unbelievable."

His eyes focused on the ambassador's, then turned and met Elizabeth's. These people barely knew him. They might actually think Zach was involved in those fires!

"Zach's a worship pastor. Katie's a journalist. They have a kid and a dog and they're just good people!"

Elizabeth settled in the chair beside her father's.

Evan stood up.

"I need to go home. My parents...." He shuddered a little. "They won't take this well. They need to hear it from me."

Ambassador Wilford rose from his chair.

"I'll go with you. In fact, we'll take my car." He led the way to the door. Evan followed, feeling like he was in a long, dark tunnel. Looking for the light at the end of it.

He was outside before he realized he should have said goodbye to Elizabeth and apologized for ditching lunch and messing up their day.

But that was the least of his concerns.

The ambassador ushered him to the non-descript black SUV and opened the passenger door. Wordlessly, Evan climbed inside.

His mind was racing, but going nowhere. Like a stuck car, its tires spinning in a snowbank.

He blinked repeatedly and tried to focus.

His host got in, put the vehicle in reverse and turned around, then drove out the wooded driveway. Evan stared, almost unseeing, through the windshield. Moments later, they pulled into the Nelsons' drive.

He ran his fingers through his hair. Filled his lungs with air. Opened the car door.

"Wait a minute!" Ambassador Wilford scrambled out of the vehicle faster than Evan thought possible, and hurried around to stop him. "I don't know your family well, but I've known them for a long time. I'll go with you."

What could it hurt? Nothing could make this worse than it already was.

"Okay." Evan forced himself to begin walking toward the door.

It opened before they got to the porch. Mom wiped her hands

on her red apron, and Dad stood behind her, looking curiously at the SUV.

Sunshine highlighted Mom's grey hair as she smiled and greeted the ambassador. "What a nice surprise! But I thought Evan was having lunch at your house."

"Mrs. Nelson. Mr. Nelson." He smiled weakly as his gaze moved from one to the other. "May we come in? I'm afraid we have some bad news."

"Oh dear." She took a step back. "Yes, of course. Come in, please."

Her eyes flitted from him to Evan. "Where's your truck?"

They moved inside.

"It's at my place," the ambassador explained. "Can we sit down?"

Dad led the way into the living room and waited until everyone else was seated. A frown turned his mouth down, and his brown eyes never left Evan. Finally, he sat on the couch next to Mom.

"What's going on?" He asked, his gaze shifting to the ambassador.

"There's no easy way to say this." Ambassador Wilford pressed his fingertips together. "Unfortunately... your son Zach is wanted for questioning in the California fires."

Mom looked at him like she was waiting for the punchline of a joke. Dad leaned forward, then back. Then forward again. Finally, he shook his head.

"I don't understand. What are you saying? They think he has information?"

"Maybe they think he was involved. He's a person of interest."

Mom's eyes turned from the ambassador to Evan, then Dad. They filled with tears. "A *suspect?*"

"Perhaps." The ambassador nodded. "He might be arrested."

Mom gasped, then covered her mouth with her hands. Tears slipped onto her cheeks. Evan's stomach soured.

Dad leaned back into the sofa, rested his hands on his lap, and stared at the wall behind Evan. Then he rubbed his chest and drew a long breath. He clenched his jaw and closed his eyes.

The ambassador spoke softly. "I know this is a horrible moment, and I apologize for being the bearer of bad news. But there are some things we need to do right away."

Dad's eyes opened.

"You're right. Of course! We need to tell them he didn't do it!" He focused on the ambassador. "Who do we call? Or maybe you should call. You have contacts."

Mom jumped up.

"I gotta talk to Zach. Where's my phone?" Her gaze skittered around the room, landing on the cell phone on the end table. She snatched it up.

"Wait! Wait just a moment," the ambassador urged, reaching out and touching her arm.

She jerked away, wet eyes blazing. "What?"

"We need to take a minute. Think about what we're doing," he said.

Dad nodded. "He's right, Michele. Sit down."

"I will not sit down! I need to talk to my son!" She moved her fingers across the screen, then held the phone to her ear, glaring at the floor.

Evan held his breath. After a few seconds, Mom whispered an expletive and hung up.

"All circuits are busy!" She said in a sarcastic sing-song echo. She dropped back on the sofa next to Dad. "When are the phones going to work again? What are we going to do?"

All eyes turned on the ambassador.

"I think you should get an attorney," he said.

"For what?" Dad asked.

"For Zach?" Mom asked.

Evan drew a deep breath. Thank goodness Ambassador Wilford had come over to break the news to his parents. It was difficult to imagine dealing with it on his own. Plus, the ambassador could help straighten all this out. As Dad said, the man had contacts.

He knew people who knew people.

He even knew the president!

"What happened before I got here?" Alana whispered to her chief of staff.

"Updates on the California fires, airport issues, fatality estimates. Also, there's a moderate solar storm that might interfere with telecommunications later today," Jason answered. "Oh, and the president informed everyone about the terror suspect."

"So I didn't miss much," she surmised.

"All the depressing details. Looks like we're losing half of the California population, at least." He rubbed his eyes. "And the ports. Cargo ships are waiting off the coast because the ports are burning."

"What about the airports and flights?"

"Seven crashes. People are panicked about those drones. FBI never caught the suspects."

Alana's mouth gaped. "So the drones are still buzzing airports?"

"No. Maybe the perps got tired and went home. They could be back anytime, though. Nobody wants to get on an airplane."

"Can't blame them," she said.

"Exactly! Plus, that fear is actually helping relieve the airport congestion problem in the western states."

"So, the airspace is still open? On 9/11, all the planes were grounded."

"Well, nobody was flying jets into buildings this weekend, and the drones have gone away." He yawned. "Man, I am so tired!"

"You should be able to get some rest this afternoon. Other

than the hunt for our suspect, we're looking at a bunch of mop up and damage control."

"And public relations manipulation." He took a swig of coffee as Alana's national security advisor slid into the open seat on the other side of her.

Every strand of Mae Hepburn's auburn hair was perfectly in place, as usual, and she was dressed impeccably as always.

Mae, prim and proper, and Jason, relaxed to the point of almost disheveled, could not be more different. Thin and angular, she was approaching retirement. He was barely thirty, and already putting on a middle-aged spare tire.

But both were brilliant, and Alana relied on their input more than any of her other staff. They were her right hand man and her left hand woman. Or something like that.

She greeted Mae with a smile.

"How soon do you think they'll let us out of the PEOC?" she asked.

"That's just what I was coming to tell you. Over the past twelve hours, the situation has stabilized. It sounds like protocols will be relaxed sometime in the next hour."

"So we'll be able to leave the bunker?"

Mae nodded. "I believe so, yes."

"Thank goodness!" Jason stretched. "This place makes me claustrophobic!"

"It's not that bad," Alana said, although she sort of agreed with him.

"There's no windows!" He protested. "All this artificial light is bad for your brain."

Across the room, the president raised her voice over the various conversations. "Hey, everyone, can I have your attention?"

The room fell silent as eyes turned toward her.

"Thirty minutes from now, we'll be leaving the bunker. We'll be able to use the Situation Room."

A few quiet cheers went up. Basilia grinned and raised her hands. More cheers, louder this time. Including Alana's.

"I'll be giving a short speech or a press conference – my security detail and I are still arguing about the location and logistics on that –"

She was interrupted by polite laughter. "Anyway, we all need to be focused on two goals this afternoon. First, reassuring the American people. And second, catching the terrorist who started those fires. Zachary James Nelson!"

CHAPTER FOUR

Katie rushed into the motorhome.

"Zach!" She lowered her voice to avoid frightening Timothy. "I heard a siren!"

Her husband's face blanched. "Where?"

"In the distance. I'm not sure!"

"Is it coming this direction?" He moved toward the door.

"Maybe. I don't know!"

Zach zig-zagged between her and the dog, and opened the door a crack.

The siren was louder now. Definitely closer.

"What are we going to do?" Katie asked as Zach yanked the door closed, then turned the flimsy lock.

"I'm going to get dressed. You better, too, and quick!"

Timothy brought her a couple of tiny toy parts he'd found under the dinette. "Mommy! Fix it!"

"Not now, Tim. Mommy and Daddy are busy!" Katie opened the tiny closet that held their clothing. She grabbed a clean t-shirt and pair of shorts. There was no time to think about a shower.

It was just get dressed and get ready.

For what? She couldn't be sure, but she knew it'd be bad.

Zach came out of the bathroom in clean jeans and a short-sleeved button down shirt. He looked respectable. What if that outfit was what he'd be wearing on his perp walk – the one that would get replayed over and over on television and the internet, showing his arrest or march into jail or whatever?

The thought rocked her as she dressed.

She tried to pray, but could barely focus. Still, she believed the Lord heard her heart's cries.

Zach opened the RV door a little. The siren was growing fainter. It was moving away!

Katie leaned against the wall. Thank God!

"What do you think we should do?" Zach closed the door. "I mean, if Jennifer was right, I need to go straighten this out!"

If Jennifer was right? The thought spun through Katie's head. Yes, there was still a possibility... they hadn't verified what she's said... maybe Jennifer had gotten it wrong.

"Turn on the TV," she suggested. "But keep the volume down."

She didn't want Timothy to get scared. Zach clicked on the television and flipped through the channels.

"Daddy's on TV!" Timothy screeched, pointing at the screen. He jumped up and down. "Daddy! Daddy!"

Well, that answered that question. Katie moved so she could see the screen, too. Zach muted it so Timothy wouldn't hear the details, but she and Zach read the chyron under his photo.

"Nice picture," she muttered.

"It's the one from my driver's license," he said.

"I've seen enough. You?"

"Yep." He flicked it off, and turned to stare at her. "How in the world...?"

She shook her head. "I have no idea. It's so crazy!"

"Should I get an attorney? Go to a police station?" He ran his hands over his head. "How do I make this go away?"

How, indeed? Katie slumped against the fridge. Her stomach growled. Her brain refused to function. She reached for his hand.

"Let's pray for answers."

After she muddled her way through a prayer, Zach squeezed her hand.

"We need to get out of here."

"What?" Her eyes focused on his. "Not get an attorney? Just run?"

"I'm not running, I'm just... I need some time to think!"

"But –" She didn't know how to object to that. After all, it's not like things could get any worse. He was already in the worst position possible. Suspected of launching a terror attack that destroyed the state of California. So what if they added some kind of fleeing charge on top of that? It couldn't make any difference! Could it?

Evan turned his attention to the ambassador.

"Maybe you could call the president," he suggested. "Tell her Zach didn't do this."

Ambassador Wilford pursed his lips. A doubtful look flitted across his face, then disappeared.

"I don't know," he said, turning old blue eyes toward Evan. "We don't have any proof of his innocence yet."

Dad rose from the couch. "This is America! Nobody has to prove their innocence!"

"It would help to have an alibi, though," the ambassador said. "But with the phone networks overwhelmed right now...."

"There's nothing we can do." Dad paced toward the window, then back to the sofa. "There must be something!"

Mom stood up and stepped toward him. "We should go home. In Baltimore, we can access attorneys and media and people who could help. Here in the sticks, there's nothing."

The ambassador cocked his head.

"What brought you out to Galloway this weekend, anyway?"

Dad turned and looked at Mom. Then Evan. His Adam's apple bobbed as he swallowed.

"Zach." His word was barely more than a whisper.

Evan jumped in. "He was worried about what was going on. He called me yesterday and told me about the fires, and suggested we leave the city for the rest of the weekend. Just in case."

The ambassador fixed him with a stare. "In case of what?"

"I don't know, he – he's one of those people who always worries about the end of the world as we know it," Evan said. "So he figured if the west coast was attacked, maybe the rest of the country would be, too... I don't know."

Was he making Zach look bad? He wasn't trying to. He was only trying to explain his brother's thought processes.

"So you're here because he warned you," the ambassador said.

"Yes, but nothing happened. Here, I mean," Evan added. "He was evacuating his family from the fires when he called."

Their guest took a sip of water and swallowed it slowly.

Dad sat back down. "What are you thinking?"

Ambassador Wilford's gaze dropped to the floor.

"It's probably nothing."

"What's nothing?" Mom asked, turning worried eyes on the man.

"Well, playing devil's advocate here, not that I think this, but the FBI or prosecutors –"

"What?" Mom stared at him. "WHAT?"

"Okay. Look at it this way. If he was involved – and I don't believe he was – but if he was, it could make sense that he'd contact you and encourage you to leave town."

"Why?" Dad asked.

"Because as soon as his face appeared on internet and TV, hordes of media would show up at your home." The ambassador gave them a very serious look. "In fact, you could be in danger."

"Us?" Mom asked. "Why?"

"The state of California was torched. Millions have died already, and more millions will die over the next few days. That's going to leave a lot of grieving, angry people looking for revenge on whomever they believe caused it."

"But Zach didn't –" Evan interjected.

"But his name and photo are on TV!" Mom's eyes filled with tears. She clasped her hands together.

"What should we do?" Dad asked the ambassador.

"For one thing, I don't think you should go home. I still think you should hire an attorney, but since this is Sunday and the phones aren't working..." He shook his head. "To be honest, I'm just not sure."

Alana glanced over as Basilia approached. The president spoke quietly, just above a whisper.

"So, you never did tell me what the ambassador to Israel wanted when he called in the middle of the night."

"Right. It was pretty odd-ball, actually. About an ancient Jewish prophecy."

"Are you kidding me?" Basilia pushed her glossy black hair over her shoulder.

"Nope. The prophecy foretold a young country at the end of the world that would betray Israel and then that country would be destroyed in a single day. Something like that."

Basilia recovered from a momentary shudder.

"That's crazy talk," she said. "He really needs to retire."

"Maybe you should suggest it," Alana said, then quickly changed the subject. "How's your family?"

"They're fine. Squawking a little about extra security measures and bunkers, but they should just be glad they're safe."

"Dominic and the kids are coming back tonight?"

"Yes. School in the morning." Basilia glanced at her watch. "I need to go over my speech. Would you get an update from the FBI on our manhunt?"

"Sure."

The president floated toward the far end of the room, where her chief of staff and speechwriter huddled over a computer. Alana poured herself a steaming cup of coffee before cornering Dick Chalmers, the FBI director. At least thirty years her senior, with steel grey hair and brown eyes, he was trim and fit and looked like he hadn't lost a minute's sleep last night.

"Where are we at with locating our terrorist?" she asked.

"Should have him within the hour."

"Good." She pursed her lips. Should she tell him her idea about having him knocked off?

No. She didn't know him well enough. She'd have to find someone she could trust. And drop a hint very carefully. Deniably.

"You have his exact location, then?" Alana pressed.

"Essentially, yes. We're moving assets into place as we speak."

Something in his eyes troubled her. It was like nobody was home. Like there was no life in them.

"Good." She took a sip of her scalding brew and turned away.

Not a lot of people had truly creepy eyes, but that man sure did!

Grace Denver, the president's chief of staff, clapped her hands twice to get everyone's attention.

"Okay, people! Good news – we're done down here. We can head up to the Situation Room!"

"Finally!" Jason grabbed his laptop and briefcase.

The room burst into a flurry of activity as everyone gathered their belongings. Alana set her coffee down. Since the security protocols were relaxed, maybe she'd step outside for a minute. Get a breath of fresh air and a moment of sunshine.

This bunker life was for the birds!

CHAPTER FIVE

Zach said he wasn't running, but it sure felt like it to Katie. She got Timothy dressed, buckled him in his car seat at the dinette table, and gave him breakfast while Zach prepared the motorhome for takeoff and fed Duke. They were actually ready to roll in less than five minutes. A new record.

They settled in the front seats of the RV to make a plan. Sunlight washed through the windows and warmed Katie's knees.

"Where are we going to go?" she asked. "North, south or east? Certainly not back west!"

"Reno?" Zach asked. "It's not far, and we could get lost in a city that size."

"You really don't think we should turn ourselves in?" Katie asked. It felt so wrong to run when you knew the cops wanted to talk to you.

Zach leaned close and whispered, "What do you think will happen to Timothy?"

She gulped. What *would* happen to him? They didn't have any relatives nearby who could watch him. Her parents were in Costa Rica, her sister was in Canada, and Zach's brother and parents were clear across the country, in Baltimore. Or perhaps West

Virginia, if they'd bugged out to their summer cabin like Zach had asked them to yesterday.

No, Timothy would fall into the hands of the state foster care system if she and Zach were arrested. And that was absolutely unacceptable!

Would she be arrested, too, or just Zach? Supposedly they were looking for him, but they'd try to connect her as well. As an accomplice. Or they'd get her for fleeing, or not turning Zach in, or something. No, she had to expect that if he were arrested, she would be also. Particularly if they were found together.

"Maybe we should split up," she blurted.

"What?" Zach's blazing blue eyes locked on hers. "Why?"

"So they don't take Timothy," she whispered.

Instantly, she regretted suggesting it. She didn't want to split up! Today of all days, she needed her little family together. All of them.

"Maybe," he mused, turning his gaze out the windshield.

"No, I don't want to! It's a bad idea. I'm sorry I even brought it up!" She reached for his hand. "We're in this together."

He squeezed her fingers. "So. We'll all hang together, or we'll hang separately?"

She appreciated the reference to Benjamin Franklin's comments as the Continental Congress prepared to sign the Declaration of Independence, but she didn't smile.

"Yes," she whispered. Looking at him, she added, "Reno it is, then."

They said a quick but earnest prayer. Then Katie gave him a kiss, got out of the Minnie Winnie, and walked over to the pickup. She glanced at the damaged bumper from yesterday's nasty truck driver. It wasn't too terrible.

And today, at least, she had gas in the tank!

She started the pickup and followed Zach out of the hotel parking lot and back onto the highway. Her shoulders slumped.

The Sunday morning weather was perfect, but this day could turn out to be the worst one of her life.

Even worse than yesterday, if that was possible!

As they drove east toward Reno, traffic grew heavier.

And so did Katie's heart. What were they thinking, running from the police? That would never turn out well.

The whole U.S. government and most of the country would be looking for them. Or for Zach, anyway. She wasn't sure if her own photo had been splashed across the news and internet. But if it hadn't yet, it would be soon.

People would find all her messages and photos on social media, and they'd go viral.

She palmed her forehead. They needed to delete their social media accounts. All of them! Right now!

She called Zach. And got the "circuits busy" message. She hung up and picked up the walkie talkie.

"Zach?"

She needed to think of a code name for him. Saying his real name over the radio waves seemed like a bad idea.

"Yeah?"

"Don't say my name! I won't say yours anymore, either."

Silence.

"We need to pull over as soon as you find a good place. I need to delete some stuff."

"Can't it wait?"

"Social media," she said, hoping he'd get the idea.

"Oh! Right." He paused. "I'll stop soon."

"Good. Out."

About a dozen more miles ticked by as they drove along I-80 towards Reno. Finally, they approached a rest area, and Zach signaled a turn into the entrance. Katie followed him into the truck parking area, and pulled up behind him.

She scrambled out of the pickup and jogged to the RV. Duke

met her at the door, with a huge wag of his whole body. She rubbed his ears, smiled at her son, and looked toward Zach.

"We need to get rid of our social media accounts! People are going to look for them, and –"

"I know." He pulled out his phone. "Can't we just make them private?"

"No! One of our *friends* would sell us out for enough money. Too many people already have access. Distant cousins, old college acquaintances, former co-workers...."

"You're right." His fingers swiped across his screen as Katie went to work on her own accounts.

It seemed to take forever. Finally, though, they were pretty sure they'd deleted or inactivated all their accounts.

"What a pain!" Katie rolled her eyes. At least it was done, though.

Her stomach growled. She'd fed Timothy, but totally forgot to eat anything herself. She grabbed a banana.

"Want one?"

Zach and Timothy both nodded. Duke licked his chops.

"Not you, silly!" She bypassed the giant dog to hand out fruit to the guys.

As she peeled her banana, she turned on the television. Zach's image appeared. Not his driver's license photo this time. A different one, and she was in it, too! It was a photo from last year's vacation to Yosemite. She'd posted it online for her friends.

Someone, maybe at a news agency or even her own employer, had scraped their personal information before she and Zach had taken down their accounts.

"I guess we were too late." She hung her head. If only they'd never posted on stupid social media!

Evan leaned back in his chair. His gaze slid from the ambassador to his mom, then to Dad. What on earth were they going to do?

If only they could reach Zach!

He pulled out his cell phone and tried calling.

Still couldn't get through.

Mom sank onto the sofa beside Dad. Tears leaked onto her cheeks.

"We've got to do *something*!" She looked at Evan, then at the ambassador.

Their guest stroked his chin, staring at the carpet. Hopefully coming up with a genius plan. Evan picked up the remote and turned on the television. He only needed to flip two channels before Zach's picture came on the screen. It was probably a driver's license photo, but someone had tweaked the colors and somehow made it look more like a mug shot.

"Turn it up!" Mom said.

Evan adjusted the volume so they could all hear the reporter.

"Zachary James Nelson, 31, of California, is wanted for questioning in the terrorist fires," the reporter said. "He was last seen fleeing the state towards Reno, Nevada. He's believed to be armed and dangerous –"

"That's a lie!" Mom yelped.

" – and citizens are asked to report his location, but not approach him."

Dad's face reddened. "Turn it off!"

Evan clicked the remote. The image faded into black as the screen darkened. His mouth went dry.

This was for real.

His brother, good ol' Zach the worship pastor, was really suspected in the fires that even now were consuming the great state of California and much of its population.

How did this happen? How had the authorities come to think Zach was involved?

And was there any possibility – any at all – that it might be true?

No! He shook his head. No, that was impossible.

Wasn't it?

But something, somehow, had sparked the FBI's interest in him. Something had caused suspicion. What could it have been?

Zach was a good guy. He'd always stayed out of trouble.

Sure, he was a bit of a Bible-thumper, but he wouldn't hurt a fly.

And certainly wouldn't hurt a person. Or a whole state full of them.

Somehow, Evan had to figure out what the investigators were thinking. And then, somehow, he had to convince them they were on the wrong track. But how? How could he do that?

And if they were convinced that Zach was involved, what was to prevent them from thinking he was, too? What if he became a suspect simply because he was Zach's little brother?

Nah. That was crazy!

Wasn't it?

On the south lawn, Alana closed her eyes and tilted her chin toward the sun. Warmth flooded her face. She inhaled deeply, breathing in the autumn air. Birds chirped in the nearest trees.

Another perfect September day!

She exhaled.

Well, perfect if you hadn't heard about what was happening in California.

Fighting the temptation to take off her shoes and walk barefoot in the grass, she turned back to the White House. It looked glorious in the sun, bastion of power and freedom.

Especially now that Basilia resided here. The progressives'

dream had finally come true. They had placed a committed socialist in the seat of world domination.

And *she* was Basilia's VP! It was still hard to believe.

Smiling, she stepped onto the shaded portico, ignoring her security detail. She made her way quickly to the Situation Room, where everyone who mattered was assembling. Except the president.

"Where's Basilia?" Alana whispered to Jason.

"Getting ready to give her statement." He ran pudgy fingers through his untamed hair.

"In the press briefing room?"

"Yep." He picked up a remote and turned on a television screen.

An image of the packed briefing room came on, with a female reporter's voice-over.

"Moments from now, President Hernandez will be giving an update on this weekend's events in California," the journalist said over the quiet buzz of other voices in the room. "The mood here is somber, anxious and grieving."

She paused, then spoke in a hushed voice. "I believe the president is just about to make her appearance."

CHAPTER SIX

Katie watched the television news in the motorhome, while Zach took Timothy to the men's room in the rest area.

She shuddered as she watched the morning video footage of the California fires. Whole cities had gone up in flames overnight. It was unbelievable.

And they were blaming Zach for it?

Her head shook. That was so crazy!

Maybe he should just turn himself in. What if the FBI located Zach, and some trigger-happy cop shot him?

Her eyes widened. That wasn't so far-fetched! Stuff like that actually happened these days.

The RV door swung open, and Zach hoisted Timothy into the motorhome. He looked upset.

"People are looking at me funny. Let's get out of here!"

She turned off the television. "Are you sure?"

"Sure, I'm sure! I'm not getting out of the RV anymore. I'll use our own facilities!" He slid into the driver's seat. "Let's move."

She scrambled out of the motorhome and back to the pickup, glancing at passersby. No one looked at her funny.

"Yet," she muttered. Her pictures were on TV now, too. And the internet, no doubt.

She started the Ford and followed the motorhome back onto the interstate.

Zach was right, he should stay in the vehicle from now on.

Until when? Was he going to stay in there for the rest of his life? Was the government going to miraculously realize they'd made a major mistake, and stop looking for him? Why would that happen?

Did he think he could run forever? Did he think it would all blow over?

What was he thinking, anyway?

Or maybe, he just needed *time* to think, as he'd said.

He did. And she did, too.

And to pray.

Sorry, Lord, that was my last thought. Katie sighed. Please help us. Again.

If only she could get some good advice! Her dad would know what to do. He always did. But he was in Costa Rica now. And her phone wasn't working.

If only she and Zach had moved down there with her parents! They had extra bedrooms, and extended the invitation to help them move and get on their feet down there.

If they'd taken advantage of her parents' offer, all of this craziness would have been avoided. They wouldn't have spent yesterday nearly getting overrun by fire, and they wouldn't be spending this morning running from the FBI.

Instead, they'd be having a leisurely weekend on some sandy beach, and attending her parents' church.

If only.

Too bad she couldn't turn back the clock. Get her family safely moved to the tropics. Lounge in a hammock, sipping iced tea.

Well, they'd brought their passports with them when they'd

evacuated yesterday. But it'd be impossible to get on a flight now. Even if they could somehow get tickets, they'd never make it through security. Alarms would go off all over. Men with guns would come rushing at them, taking her and Zach to jail and Timothy to God-knows-where.

She blinked back tears. No, they were stuck here in the United States, with the government looking for them.

How long would it take them to find her family? How could they possibly hide?

She picked up the walkie talkie.

"Zach?" She cringed. She couldn't keep saying his name over the radio!

"Yes."

"I have an idea. But we need to stop for a few minutes and discuss something."

As they entered Reno, traffic was heavy, but there were lots of places to pull off.

"Okay. But let's make it quick." Zach signaled a turn at the upcoming off-ramp, and Katie tucked in behind him. He pulled into a huge shopping mall. The parking lot was half-empty.

Katie parked the pickup and walked over to his open window.

"We should decide where we're going, then leave hints that we're going somewhere else," she said.

"And you can't use my name on the walkie talkie!" Zach protested. "We need code names. How about Runner and Mermaid?"

Katie almost smiled. Zach was a runner, now in more ways than one. And everyone who knew her, knew she'd always loved the water.

"Fine." She lowered her sunglasses and looked over the lenses at him. "Now, where do you want to go?"

Evan wiped his damp palms on his pants, trying to sort out what to do... or not do. The ambassador was right; going back to Baltimore this afternoon was out of the question. No doubt media would be staking out his home, and his parents' place.

Should he contact the FBI? Or lay low here in Galloway, and hope nobody came looking?

Realistically, he knew it was inevitable that somebody would come looking. His father's name was on the title for this property. They'd turn that up soon enough.

Besides, if the authorities wanted to find them, they'd just ping their cell phones and know right where they were.

Would the FBI think they were all hiding out in the boonies because they were accomplices?

His gaze shifted to the ambassador, who silently stared at the floor. Hopefully he was lost in thought, coming up with a brilliant idea. Mom sniffled into her tissue, while Dad sat beside her and rubbed her shoulder.

Evan frowned. If only he could talk to Zach!

He could at least send a text or leave a message. Eventually, Zach should get it. He reached for his cell phone. What would he say? What *should* he say?

Anything he said or wrote could become evidence in some future trial – against Zach, or against himself!

Still, he wanted to reach out, to connect somehow with his brother. That guy must be scared out of his wits by now, if he knew what was being said about him.

His fingers hovered over the phone. Finally, he sent a neutral text.

Call me. ASAP!!!

That shouldn't get anyone in trouble.

Finally, Mom spoke up.

"We'd planned to go home today, so I didn't pick up many groceries. If we think we're going to stay a little longer, maybe I should go to the store."

"Are you thinking of going to Clarksburg?" Dad asked.

"There's a little market in Simpson," the ambassador said. "Spencer's Market. If you don't want to drive clear to Clarksburg."

Mom rose from the sofa, twisting her hands. "I just need to do *something!*"

"Maybe you could top off the gas tank, too," Dad said. "So we won't have to do that later."

"Okay." She looked at Evan. "You want to drive?"

He nodded.

"Sure. But I left the pickup at the ambassador's home." He'd brought his parents out from Baltimore in the quad-cab, so it was the only vehicle available. "I'll walk over and get it."

"I could drive you," Ambassador Wilford offered.

"No, that's okay. I could use the fresh air," Evan said. "Plus, maybe you and Dad can come up with a plan."

"We'll certainly try."

Evan headed out the door, walked down the driveway, and started toward the ambassador's cabin. He should probably say something to Elizabeth before he got in the truck and drove off.

As he walked in her driveway, he tried to think of what to say. But when he knocked on the door, and she answered it, he found himself at loss for words. Again.

"Hi."

"Hello." She glanced past him. "Where's Dad?"

"He's still with my parents. I just came back to get my truck."

"Oh. Okay."

"And I'm sorry about lunch."

She gave him a sympathetic smile. "Don't worry about it."

He moved back from the door. "Maybe I'll see you around?"

"Maybe you will." Another smile, then she closed the door and he was left alone on the porch.

Barely breathing.

She was simply the most perfect creature he'd ever seen.

Next thing he knew, he was in his truck, and then he was

parking it at his family's summer cabin. Mom came out the door before he climbed out of the pickup. Her purse was tucked under her arm, and her mouth was set in a grim line.

Alana took her seat as she watched the television.

On-screen, the camera panned to the entryway, and Basilia stepped into the briefing room and up to the podium. The camera zoomed to her face. Tiredness lined her sad eyes, but she held her head high, her chin up.

Her shoulders lifted slightly as she inhaled, sweeping the room with her gaze. She exhaled, rested her hands on the podium, and glanced at the teleprompter.

"My fellow Americans, today is a day of mourning. Evil has assaulted our great nation and stolen the lives of millions of our friends and neighbors. Our American family is reeling."

Barely breathing herself, Alana stared at the screen. Basilia paused, turned her eyes to the other teleprompter, and continued.

"But know this –" she raised a finger for emphasis – "those who perpetrated this unspeakable act will be caught. They will be punished! The remainder of their short lives will be lived in infamy!"

Complete silence emanated from her captivated audience.

"And hear me now. The United States will come together to weather this travesty. We stand united against hate and bigotry. And California will rise from the ashes! She will come back stronger –"

Basilia suddenly looked to her left.

Something was happening off-screen, and Alana couldn't tell what was going on. Was there a disruption? A threat?

Alana stood up, knocking over a glass of water, as the camera zoomed out, showing the entire podium area and the entire front of the room.

Men – Secret Service agents – rushed the president, grabbing her and pulling her from the lectern.

Alana's hand flew to her mouth. What was going on?

The agents half-dragged, half-carried the president out of the briefing room, which erupted into confusion and chaos. Alana almost expected the press secretary to make an appearance and explanation, but no official came to the podium.

The spilled ice water was running across the table toward her laptop.

"I need a towel!" She looked up as agents rushed into the Situation Room. Several beelined toward her, while others moved toward other members of the president's cabinet.

Before she could protest, she was lifted off her feet and rushed through the door.

Here we go again!

They raced her down the hall, around a corner, into a disguised stairway, and down, down, down toward the bunker.

This time, she didn't resist. It'd do no good anyway. It'd only serve to scuff up her shoes.

CHAPTER SEVEN

Katie stood next to Zach's rolled-down window.

"I want to go someplace where we can lay low for a while," he said, glancing past her.

She nodded. "Idaho?"

"Yeah, maybe. Or Montana or Wyoming."

"So we'll head east for sure. We can stay on I-80. But first, we need to mislead anybody who's tracking us." Katie searched her husband's eyes. "How about if we detour to the south side of Reno, like we're headed to Carson City, top up our gas tanks somewhere south of the airport, then veer northeast and reconnect with I-80 east of Reno and Sparks?"

"Sounds good to me. After that, we'll have to stop using our credit cards. How much cash do we have?"

"Thousands. I cleaned out our safe when we evacuated," Katie said.

His eyebrows narrowed. "I'm sorry we're going to have to use some of that. I know you were saving it for our tenth anniversary bash."

"Or for a rainy day," she reminded him.

He leaned out his window and kissed her. "You're the best."

She smiled. "We should get going. You want to lead, since you're driving the beast?"

"That'd be good. Getting into a gas station with this monster isn't always easy."

"Pick a station that looks best to you," she said.

She returned to the pickup and followed him through Reno traffic. As they neared the airport, she tensed. There were a lot of cop cars in the area!

Maybe this wasn't such a good idea after all.

When Zach finally pulled into a gas station, she jumped out of the truck and ran toward him. By the time she reached him, he was already standing at the pump with his credit card. He slid his card into the reader.

"WAIT!"

He turned toward her. He'd put on a Seahawks baseball cap, which he'd pulled low over his eyes. Good thinking.

"Don't use the card!" She panted as she reached him.

"Why? I thought that was the whole idea!" His eyebrows drew together. "So they'd think we were going south, when we're not."

"Maybe I was wrong," she said. "There's too many cops around here. If the FBI is monitoring our credit cards in real time, they can probably have police here in less than ten minutes!"

Zach yanked out his card and canceled the transaction.

"If it didn't actually make a charge, do you think they'll still see it?" He pushed the card back into his wallet.

"I don't know!" Katie looked toward the street.

What if the police were already on the way?

"We can fill up and pay with cash," he said.

The hair on the back of her neck tingled.

"I think we should get out of here. Right now! How much gas do you have?"

"At least a half tank."

"Me, too." Her eyes met his. "Please, can we just leave? We can top up with cash somewhere along the way."

"Fine." He walked around the RV and opened the driver side door.

She hustled back to the pickup. Moments later, they pulled out onto the street.

Being back in the vehicle brought a little relief to her anxiety. For some reason, that gas station creeped her out. She just wanted to get away from there, as quickly as possible. Without drawing attention.

Zach drove a course that took them northeast, toward Sparks, as they'd planned.

Katie noticed a police car at an intersection ahead. Was he waiting there for them?

Evan opened the pickup door for his mom, then returned to the driver's side and climbed in, started the engine, and pulled out of the driveway.

"Do you want to try the little market, or go to Clarksburg?" he asked.

Mom pursed her lips. "Clarksburg, I guess. They have a branch of my bank there, and I can get some cash from the ATM."

As they passed the ambassador's driveway, Evan couldn't help looking. And his mother caught him doing it.

"She's still single, you know." Mom gave him a pointed look.

Evan tried to avoid it by focusing on the road ahead.

"You should ask her out. Before it's too late."

"Mom!" He glanced her way. "Are you kidding me right now? We have a crisis! Zach's in big trouble."

"You think I forgot that?" Her eyes got all watery. "No! I'm just trying to lighten the mood, is all."

She pointed her trembling chin at him. "Plus, you could do a lot worse. She's a nice girl and she won't be on the market for long."

"Let it go, Mom."

"Whatever." She gave him a dismissive wave of her hand. "You snooze, you lose."

He bit his lip to keep his mouth shut. She'd always get in the last word. Better to let her have it now, rather than prolong the misery by continuing down this conversational path.

It seemed like it took longer than normal to drive to Clarksburg, but eventually they arrived and Evan drove her to her bank. He parked on the street in front of the building and waited as she got out. Several people were in line at the ATM, which seemed odd, given that it was a Sunday afternoon.

After a few minutes, she returned with her cash.

"Good thing we stopped here first," Mom said as she climbed into the pickup. "The lady ahead of me said the grocery store isn't taking credit cards."

"Why not?" He put the truck into gear and signaled his turn into traffic.

"Something about the internet or phone lines."

He shifted back into park and turned off the truck.

"What are you doing?" Mom looked at him.

"Maybe I should get some cash, too." He reached for his wallet.

"I got enough," she said. "I'm only getting a few groceries. Not a month's worth!"

"Yeah, well..." Truth was, he had a funny feeling in his gut. "I'm low on cash myself. Might as well get some now."

Exiting the pickup, he joined the line at the ATM.

There were two grannies ahead of him, and they took their sweet time. Maybe trying to remember their PINs or something. After an eternity, they finally finished. By then, five more people had lined up behind Evan.

He stepped up, slid his card into the slot, and pressed the buttons for $300.

The display promptly informed him the cash wasn't available. *What?*

He tried $200.

Still no dice.

One hundred dollars?

The machine spit out his money, receipt and card.

Walking back to the pickup, he put everything in his wallet. Had the bank lowered the cash limit? Or was the machine out of money because half the town was lining up to get some?

At least he got a little.

Back in the truck, he pulled onto the street and headed for the grocery store.

"How much money did you get?" He asked, glancing at Mom.

"Two hundred. Why?"

"It'd only give me one hundred. I think we drained it." He turned into the grocery store parking lot.

The only empty parking spaces were those farthest from the front doors. Who knew Sunday afternoon was the time the entire town went grocery shopping?

Evan found an empty space and nosed the truck into it, cramming in between a Suburban and a minivan. A parade of vehicles followed him in from the street and soon filled up the remaining parking spaces.

What on earth was going on?

The agents deposited Alana unceremoniously back in the Presidential Emergency Operations Center. The president was already there, smoothing her skirt and glaring at her Secret Service detail.

"What the –"

"There's been a bomb, Ma'am," an agent said, stepping out of Basilia's reach.

"Couldn't you have waited thirty more seconds?" Her eyes burned into him. "I was almost finished. That stunt you pulled just played out on national television!"

"No, Ma'am," he said, then added, "Yes, Ma'am."

Her fingers curled into fists.

"Where was the bomb?" She demanded.

"New York City, Ma'am."

Alana's heart flip-flopped. She – and the president – had just been there last night! They'd been planning to be there today!

Had they been targeted?

"What kind of bomb?" Basilia asked, each word carefully clipped.

"We were told it was nuclear, Madam President."

Alana choked. WHAT?

NYC had been nuked?

No. Not possible. They'd *just* been there!

As her eyes turned to the president, Basilia launched into a tirade of curses. Seconds ticked by as more cabinet members were ushered into the PEOC, where the president of the United States was turning the air blue.

Time slowed. Alana's jaw hung loose.

Every moment clicked by like a camera shutter, etching each split second into her mind as individual images she'd never forget.

Her breath rasped into her lungs.

She gripped the table to steady herself, then eased into a chair.

New York.

Nuked.

How? Why? *Who?*

CHAPTER EIGHT

As she approached the intersection with the police car, Katie couldn't get her shoulders to relax. Was he expecting them? Looking for them?

Had Zach actually triggered the credit card tracking when he'd inserted his card into the gas pump, even though he'd canceled the transaction?

Had surveillance video from the gas station been reviewed already, and was there an alert for their motorhome?

Zach's brake lights came on. His traffic light was red. The police officer's light must be green.

Would he proceed on his way?

Or would he spot them and pull them over?

What if he didn't know they were in two vehicles? Would he pull Katie over, thinking Zach was in the pickup with her?

If he did, she hoped Zach would just keep driving.

But what if he pulled Zach over?

She wouldn't want to go anywhere without him. And their son!

No, if Zach got pulled over, she'd stop, too. They'd all hang together, as Benjamin Franklin had said.

Katie came to a stop at the light behind Zach. Finally, the police car began to pull forward. Katie expelled a breath she hadn't realized she'd been holding.

Thank you, Lord. She glanced up. Please, get us out of here!

The officer moved on down the street, and Katie rubbed the knots in her shoulders.

How soon could they get out of this town? It was crawling with cops! She pictured the interstate across Nevada, with its miles and miles of empty landscape and little traffic and fewer patrol vehicles, and couldn't wait to get there.

The city felt dangerous, even on this beautiful sunny morning.

The sooner they got out of there, the better!

Her phone buzzed.

What? The phones were working?

As their light turned green and traffic began moving, Katie rustled through her bag for the phone. Finding it, she pulled it out. Dozens of text messages were finally coming in, including one from her brother in law back east. But she didn't dare read them yet.

She focused on the traffic ahead, and on getting out of this town.

As soon as she could, she'd read and reply to them all. As soon as this was all behind them.

After what seemed like eons, she finally saw a sign for I-80. In a few moments, they'd be on the freeway!

"Thank God," she breathed. "Thank you, thank you!"

As they approached the on-ramp, Zach signaled his turn, and Katie followed suit.

But as the motorhome moved into the lane, she had a sickening thought. Their cell phones were working again – so couldn't the government ping the phones to locate Zach?

They needed to get rid of them, right away!

The motorhome lumbered up the ramp and picked up speed

to merge with the interstate traffic as Katie reached for her walkie talkie.

"Runner. Come in, Runner."

Nothing but static. Zach merged into the travel lane, and Katie signaled and watched her mirrors to do the same.

"Runner! Are you there, Runner?"

She slid the pickup in between a Corvette and a minivan. The motorhome was now three vehicles ahead.

"Runner?"

Why wasn't he responding? Had he turned off the walkie talkie? Maybe switched channels by accident?

She looked at her own. It seemed fine.

Well, the phones were working, apparently. She could try calling him.

But – would that somehow draw attention to their location? No, it probably didn't matter. The cell towers pinged all the phones in range, so if the system was functional, the authorities should know exactly where Zach was. Or where his phone was, anyway. And which way he was headed.

So why hadn't they picked him up?

Maybe if the phones had just come back online, the towers were only just now able to ping them again?

Katie didn't know.

All she knew was, they needed to ditch those phones.

ASAP.

And she hadn't been able to reach Zach on the walkie talkie.

She reached for her phone. Made the call. Listened while it rang. And rang. And rang.

Evan got out of the pickup and waited for his mother. As she came around the truck, her gaze swept all the vehicles in the lot.

"Looks like we picked a bad time." She put on her sunglasses.

"Yeah, I guess." He suspected there was more to it than bad timing. Maybe the store was having a huge Sunday sale? Maybe people were nervous because of the California attacks, and they wanted their pantries to be stocked up if anything else happened. That's what they did on 9/11, after all.

They made their way into the store, but there were no shopping carts. Mom's shoulders drooped as she looked despairingly at the cart area.

"I'll just get a hand basket," she said.

But the basket bin was empty, too.

"Wait here." Evan started back outside. "I'll get you a cart."

In the parking lot, a lady near the entrance had just emptied her cart.

"I can get that for you," he offered with a smile, reaching for the cart.

"Oh!" She glanced at him. "Thanks."

He wheeled the cart inside, and soon Mom had it half-filled with groceries. He grabbed some jerky, shaving cream, and toothpaste.

Every aisle was packed with shoppers, which made the whole experience take twice as long as it should have. And twice as much hassle. After an eternity, they finally joined the lines at the checkout counters.

He'd never been in a line this long. Seriously! At least half the town was in this one line!

It took twenty-two minutes to get to the cashier. He knew, because he timed it.

"We're only taking cash," she said in a monotone as he started placing goods on the conveyer belt.

"That's fine."

About his age, the blonde cashier might have been pretty once, but she'd destroyed her looks. Crazy tattoos covered her arms down to her wrists, and she'd stretched holes at least an inch in diameter in her ear lobes. A ring jutted from her lower lip.

Totally un-kissable.

Robotically, she began scanning their groceries.

He felt sorry for her. She could ditch the facial piercing, but those full sleeves and her ears would only get uglier with each passing year. Didn't she know that?

"That'll be $114.63," she said.

Mom pulled money from her purse, and Evan handed her a twenty for his purchases. She got change, and he pushed the cart toward the door.

Finally! They had their groceries and could get out of this place.

A red-haired teenaged girl came running into the store just as he was maneuvering his way out. She nearly crashed into his cart, but pivoted and then skittered toward another girl loitering by the cart area.

"Did you hear?" She yelled at her friend. "New York got bombed!"

"Yeah, duh... everybody knows that. Why do you think the store's so busy?" She looped her arm through the red-head's and pulled her toward the candy display.

Evan stopped in his tracks.

New York? What?

He looked at Mom. She stared at him, wide-eyed.

Some young fool with a cart full of beer ran right into his ankle.

Alana sucked in her breath and gripped the table top. If New York got nuked, which city would get hit next? Were there, right at this instant, bombs going off all across the country? Would one land on the White House?

Was there any possibility this was all a mistake? That Secret Service got it wrong?

No, of course not – that was silly.

This had happened. They just needed to find out how bad it was, and if there were any additional attacks.

What about her family?

Her parents were in Maine, and her sister Candace was in Texas. Had they followed her instructions last night, and stocked up on food, water and fuel?

If not, they were going to regret it.

Surely Alana could use her position to make sure they were protected. That would have to wait for a while, though. Right now, her entire focus had to be on New York.

Time suddenly resumed its usual speed, and Alana shook the confusion from her head. What did they need to do first? Gather intel.

Her national security advisor, Mae Hepburn, and the president's NSA were escorted into the PEOC together. The director of Homeland Security was not even ten steps behind them, with the Secretary of Defense on his heels. The CIA director arrived. FBI Director Dick Chalmers entered moments later, shaking off his security detail.

Okay, the team was here.

And the president had stopped swearing.

Now they could all get down to business.

"Information, people!" Basilia's piercing black eyes swept the room. "Who did this? How? And are there more bombs?"

"So far, we only have reports of the one bomb in New York," the Defense secretary said.

"Was it Russia?" She asked. "North Korea?"

"Too soon to tell, Madam President."

"Was it dropped from a plane? Was it an ICBM?" Basilia's fist hit the table. "I want answers, people! Now!"

The room erupted into noise and chaos as calls were made, discussions grew heated, and arguments began.

Alana, though, sat still. An ICBM? Surely not. Even with the moderate solar storm, there were plenty of sensors that still would have picked up on an incoming intercontinental ballistic missile.

At the moment, she truly didn't know what to do. The people who could get answers quickest were doing their best. She turned on the television, muted it so it wouldn't be too distracting, and watched the images play out in silence.

The video appeared to be shot from the bay. A classic mushroom cloud formed over Manhattan. The camera angle widened slightly, and she had to assume the photographer was on a boat that was moving away from the city.

For a moment, she thought she saw the Brooklyn bridge through the smoke and dust of the explosion. Then Ellis Island came into view, and the Statute of Liberty. Badly damaged, but still recognizable.

She looked for the One World Trade Center that had replaced the original World Trade Center towers after the 9/11 attacks, but she couldn't find it. Maybe because there was too much dust and smoke. Or maybe, like its predecessors, it had been blown to bits by terrorists.

CHAPTER NINE

Katie's call went to Zach's voice mail. Should she leave a message? What if she said something that later somehow could be construed as incriminating her, like, *Get rid of your cell phone, right now!* The last thing she wanted was to add more suspicion to either of them.

"Call me. Right away!"

She hung up. That should be fine.

But when would he get that message? After they got pulled over?

She should try to get into the adjacent lane, catch up to him and motion for him to call her. That shouldn't be too hard.

When an opening cleared in the lane to her left, she put on her blinker and moved into it. Zach was still three vehicles ahead, but her lane was moving faster than his.

Not by much, though.

It took several minutes to crawl past the first vehicle. At this rate, it could practically take half an hour to pull alongside the Minnie Winnie!

Maybe she should get into the next lane to her left. It was moving a little faster, but then she'd be two lanes over from Zach when she caught up to him. It'd be trickier to send hand signals – or impossible if something like a truck was in the lane between them.

Her phone buzzed.

It was him!

"Did you get my message?" she asked.

"Yeah. What's up? And why did you switch lanes?"

"I wanted to catch up to you! We have to do something about our phones. Take the batteries out, so the cell towers can't ping them."

"My batteries don't come out. Do yours?"

Her heart sank. No, of course they didn't. Only old-school phones had removable batteries. "No."

"Then we need to destroy the phones."

"We'll lose all our contacts," she said. "All our recent photos."

"But we have to! They can track us." He was quiet for a moment, then added, "Nobody will be able to reach us. Your family, my family...."

Katie hadn't really thought about that. Her family lived in foreign countries. Texts and calls were their primary connection.

"We can email them," she suggested.

"I think that can be tracked, too. From I.P. address locations."

Katie pulled alongside the second car behind Zach, a white Honda Civic.

"So we won't contact everybody for a little while. Just until we get this sorted out," she said. "But we absolutely have to ditch the phones."

He breathed a heavy sigh. "Fine. What do you want to do, toss 'em out the window?"

That struck her as funny. The phones would quickly get run over and destroyed, but there was also a possibility of someone's vehicle being damaged by a flying phone.

"It'd be great if we could stop at a rest area and plant them on a semi truck going the opposite direction," she said. "You know, like they do in the movies."

"It might be a while before we get to a rest area. Plus, when the phones are found, the police will have all our personal data once they get into the phones. I think we should chuck 'em!"

She rolled her eyes. "Seriously! You can't throw your phone out on the highway!"

"Why not? Littering is the least of our concerns."

That was true.

And it was unlikely that the phones would bounce and damage somebody's car.

"Okay... but I have a ton of text messages that just came through. I want to read them first."

"We'll have to stop."

"I know." Katie passed another vehicle and signaled to pull into Zach's lane behind him. "Why don't you watch for a place to get off the freeway? As soon as possible."

They were leaving the city, so fewer exits would be available. But they were in the right-hand lane, so they were in a position to take the next exit, whenever it came.

"Sounds good to me," Zach said before hanging up.

Katie clutched her phone. It had all the pictures from Timothy's fourth birthday. She hadn't downloaded them yet. And the phone numbers and contact information for all her friends and family.

She'd never bothered uploading her data to the cloud, and her phone didn't have a removable memory card. When the phone was gone, everything would be gone.

Parting with that telephone would almost be as painful as cutting off her little finger.

"Ow!" Evan rubbed his ankle and gave the guy a nasty look. "Watch where you're going!"

"Or you could not block the exit," the idiot responded, pushing his cart of beer past Evan's mom.

She had that look on her face like she was going to slap the back of the guy's head – as a child, Evan had seen that look many times when he and Zach were in trouble – but now she restrained herself.

She turned to Evan. "Let's get out of here."

"You got it." He pushed the cart out into the sunshine. Vehicles circled the parking lot like vultures, waiting for any empty parking space. Or even the possibility of one.

As they walked to the pickup, one lady in a red Tahoe actually followed them until they reached the truck, then stopped and turned on her blinker so nobody else could get their spot when they vacated it.

Evan unloaded the groceries into the back seat and rushed the cart across the lot to the cart return area. By the time he got back to the pickup, three vehicles had piled up behind the Tahoe, and one of them was honking.

"Sheesh!" He climbed in, put the truck in reverse, and headed for the street.

"I guess it's good we got here when we did," Mom said, looking over her shoulder. "What a mad house!"

They hadn't spoken a word about the bomb yet. It was like they were avoiding that topic while trying to escape the grocery store.

As they pulled onto the street, Evan turned on the radio to catch the news.

Instead, they were treated to a commercial with super-annoying voice actors.

He braked as a gas station came into view. There were lines there, too, but he'd better fill up now. He pulled in behind a pickup towing a horse trailer.

A station attendant came out of the store and began approaching each driver in the line. Several left after talking to him.

"Maybe they're out of gas?" Evan glanced toward Mom.

"Maybe we should just go home," she said.

The employee came over, and Evan rolled down his window.

"We've only got premium, and we're only taking cash."

"Okay," Evan said.

"Like paper bills," the guy clarified. "No check cards. No plastic."

"No problem." He rolled up his window as the guy walked to the next vehicle.

Good thing they'd stopped at the bank first!

"I want to go home," Mom said.

"Yeah. As soon as we fill up, we're out of here." He glanced over. Her jaw was set in her you'd-better-do-what-I-say look.

"What?" He caught her gaze. "You want to leave right now? Before we fill the tank?"

She nodded. "They just bombed New York! Who knows what they'll do next?"

"They probably won't be doing whatever it is in the boonies of Appalachia," he argued. "Plus, that's why we need to fill the tank – in case we need to go somewhere."

He pointed at the cars ahead of him in line and continued, "Because pretty soon, there won't be any gas to buy!"

The Chevy sedan ahead of him moved forward. A few more minutes, and it'd be his turn. Hopefully there would still be gas then.

"We should find shelter." Mom looked out her window, turning her eyes toward the sky. "There could be fallout."

"Mom! It was in New York!"

She focused on him. "So? You don't think the fallout will reach us here?"

"No. It won't."

"Well, how do we know the Midwest didn't get bombed, too? Maybe Columbus, Ohio? It's not that far away. There could be radiation all around us right now. It's not visible, you know!"

"But the fallout is!" He couldn't believe he was having this conversation. The worst part was, he couldn't think of anything to say that wouldn't set her off even more.

"You think you know, but you don't know," she said in her authority voice.

A half dozen retorts raced through his mind, but he knew better than to use any of them. It'd only prolong the misery.

The Chevy sedan pulled up to the pumps. He was the next vehicle in line. Finally.

Evan reached for his phone. Maybe Mom would get the idea that he wanted to be left alone.

Some texts came in, and he scrolled through them. He should contact the university about his intention to be absent tomorrow. Or maybe he should do that in the morning, instead.

There was a text from Zach, from the middle of the night. They'd escaped the fires and were safe.

He heaved a sigh. Not for long.

The feds were looking for him, and they had access to every modern surveillance technology available to man. They'd track his credit cards, ping his telephone, scan his license plates... inevitably, they'd catch him.

Did Zach know to avoid all those things? Evan swallowed. Maybe. Maybe not.

He shot off a quick text, telling his brother to ditch the cell phones and avoid interstates. Maybe it would buy him some time.

Alana took deep breaths, trying to calm the nausea that swirled her stomach. She turned to the director of Homeland Security.

"How are we going to evacuate New York?"

He shrugged. "The residents are self-evacuating, like they did on 9/11. And this time, we can't really send any help. The whole downtown is a nuclear disaster area."

Alana turned back to the television screen. Nothing but smoke, fallout and fire moved in Manhattan. Anything that had been alive there this morning was dead. Further away, maybe a few miles from the blast, people looked like ants, swarming away from ground zero.

"Shouldn't they be sheltering right now?" she asked. "They're all getting exposed to radiation!"

"Nothing we can do," the director said. "We can't communicate with them. Power and phones are all fried in that entire region."

Basilia approached them with a peculiar expression Alana couldn't quite read.

"The ambassador to Israel... what did he say last night?" The president focused her sharp eyes on her VP. Alana felt like squirming, but forced herself to remain still.

"He said there was an ancient Jewish prophecy in which a young country at the end of the world betrays Israel, and then gets destroyed."

The president sucked in her breath. "In a single day?"

"Yes." A tingle climbed Alana's neck. "You think...?"

"What if he was involved somehow?" Basilia suggested. "He called last night, and I wouldn't talk with him."

The Homeland Security director guffawed. "You think Ambassador Wilford nuked New York?!"

Alana pulled away as the president leaned forward.

"It sounds like he might have known something in advance." She motioned for the FBI director. "I want him brought in. I want to find out what he knows!"

Alana kept her mouth shut as the president talked with Director Chalmers. What was Basilia thinking? Was she going off the deep end? Being familiar with ancient prophecy had no relationship to being involved in a terrorist plot.

On the other hand, the ambassador had delayed them in D.C. yesterday morning, about the same time as the California attack was underway. And he had called with what could be certainly construed as an ominous warning last night.

Then again... what if some of those ancient seers could actually predict the future? What if the prophecy, thousands of years ago, accurately foretold the situation that the United States now found itself in?

Was the U.S. actually going to be destroyed in a single day?

Alana rose abruptly from her chair. She needed to know what exactly the prophecy said. Then she'd know if she could dismiss it out of hand, or... or what, exactly?

Where was that ambassador? Had he gone back to Israel? Or was he still here in America?

She looked at the president. "Do you want me to call the ambassador? Maybe we could get some quick answers."

"I don't know...." Basilia frowned slightly, then turned to Director Chalmers. "You think he might run if he knows we want to talk to him?"

"Only if he's guilty," the FBI director said, then appeared to reconsider. "Well, I don't know. You know him better than I do."

"Not really," Basilia admitted. "None of us know him very well. He's a leftover from President Callahan's administration, and we haven't gotten around to replacing him yet. Or getting to know him."

"Then I'd suggest you just let us show up on his doorstep. Don't call, don't let him know we're coming," Director Chalmers said. "Let's see what he does when we get there."

CHAPTER TEN

Katie followed Zach down the interstate's offramp. Several fast food restaurants lined the intersecting street, and on the next block, she saw a truck stop. Zach made his way there, and pulled up to a gas pump. Katie drove the pickup to the adjacent pump. She hopped out and hurried to his door.

"I'll go in and pay cash," she said after he rolled down the window. "If you get out to run the pumps, be sure to wear your hat."

"Because that's a great disguise," he joked.

"Keep the brim low. Or just stay in the rig, and let me do it."

"Not a chance." He reached for his hat, and Katie turned to enter the building.

She hadn't really thought he'd let her pump his gas. He'd always been down on guys who sat in their vehicle while their lady pumped gas into their rigs.

She went inside, prepaid with cash, then walked back. Zach started fueling the motorhome, then began filling the pickup's tank.

Keeping his head low, he glanced her way.

"Before we leave, we should ditch the phones here."

She sighed. “I know.”

Settling back in the pickup, she scrolled through the texts on her phone. She didn’t have time to respond to them all.

But she sent her parents a short one.

“We survived and are okay. Will be out of touch for a while, though. Pray for us.”

Zach tapped on her window, and she rolled it down.

“Tanks are topped off. You want to go get your change?”

“Sure.”

Back in the store, she was so glad she had plenty of cash. Otherwise, they’d be toast. Tracked to every purchase in every place they went. Filling the pickup wasn’t cheap, but the RV was worse. She gladly traded the cash for the anonymity, though.

She returned outside to find that Zach had pulled the motorhome off to the side of the truck stop. She drove the pickup over next to him, so her window was alongside his.

He yanked off his hat and let the breeze ruffle his blond locks. “I got the strangest text from Evan.”

“What’d he say?”

“Get rid of the cell phones, and get off the interstates.” Zach pressed his fingers against his temples. “What’s wrong with the interstates? Does he know where we are? I should call him.”

Before Katie could object, Zach placed the call and lifted the phone to his ear.

Moments later, he scowled and hung up. “Calls aren’t going through. Again.”

“The first part makes sense, anyway, and we are getting rid of our phones,” Katie said. “Do you think it’s okay to upload or download our photos first?”

“Really, I have no idea.” He frowned. “But we might not have time. I mean, they’ve likely already pinged our phones to this truck stop. They’re probably on the way here right now! Let’s just destroy them and go.”

Katie sighed. All those pictures! Timothy’s birthday....

Before she could change her mind, she got out of the truck, dropped her phone on the ground, and smashed it with her heel. Zach handed her his phone and she did the same with it.

"You better keep your walkie talkie on," she said, climbing back into the pickup. "I need to be able to talk to you."

"I will." He gave her a sad smile.

As they pulled out of the truck stop, Katie couldn't help looking up and down the street for police cars. There were no flashing lights, but a creepy feeling slithered up her back. They really needed to get out of there and find someplace to lay low.

But as Zach signaled his turn onto the freeway onramp, she wondered about his brother's warning to stay off the interstates. Why would he say that? What did he know, that they didn't?

If they were going to avoid the interstate highways, they'd have a hard time leaving the metro area. And they needed to get far, far away from here.

As quickly as possible.

After fueling up the truck, Evan drove back to Galloway as fast as he dared. He wanted to get some real news from the internet or television, and it would be good to get away from town. People were starting to get rude and pushy.

Mom was silent most of the way, which was a real change for her. Was it because of Zach, or because of the New York bombing following the heels of the California attack?

It was impossible to know, and he didn't want to ask.

As they drove past the ambassador's home, he consciously forced himself not to glance in the driveway to see if Elizabeth was in sight.

Moments later, he pulled into their own driveway – and saw Elizabeth's car parked in front of the cabin. Perhaps she'd come over to see what her dad was doing. Or bring more news.

Evan parked the pickup and grabbed a couple bags of groceries. He followed Mom into the house and straight into the kitchen. It sounded like the TV was on in the living room.

"You heard about the nuke in New York?" Dad asked, joining them.

"Only that there was a bomb." Mom put the milk in the fridge. "Was it the only one?"

"So far. And they'll never need another." Dad handed her a block of cheese from the shopping bag.

"What do you mean?" She stopped moving and searched his face.

"They hit the financial district."

A lead weight sunk in Evan's chest.

Wall Street. The stock markets. The nation's biggest banks.

All destroyed in a moment. And soaked in radioactive contamination for years.

Mom set the cheese on the counter. Her face grew unnaturally pale. She moistened her lips.

"Our retirement."

Evan picked up the cheese and put it in the fridge. Thousands of people had just been blown into nuclear ash, millions were burning in California, and her own son was at the center of the storm.

But what was her primary concern at this moment?

Her retirement.

If Alana were seventeen, she'd be chewing her fingernails. How long was it going to take for the FBI to pick up Ambassador Wilford? He had an apartment right in D.C.

Still, it felt like it was taking forever!

If he really thought the country was being destroyed, maybe he had flown to Canada or something.

Basilia beckoned her from the far end of the PEOC. Alana hurried to her side.

"This is driving me nuts – dealing with simultaneous disasters on opposite ends of the country. I need you to run point on the California fires and rounding up our terrorist, so I can focus on New York." The president's round eyes filled. "Can you do that?"

"Of course."

In fact, she was happy to be in charge of something, because she'd been feeling a little helpless, truth be told. If it'd been up to her, she would have chosen the nuke instead of the fires, but hey... she wasn't the president. Yet.

"Listen up, everybody!" Basilia waited for the room to quiet down. "We've got too much going on, so I'm delegating. Alana will be in charge of the California crisis, and I'll be handling the nuke –"

She paused. "Well, not *handling*, exactly...."

This was met with a few chuckles.

"But you know what I mean. Report to the vice president on the fire situation, and to me on the bomb."

Alana approached the FBI director.

"So where are we on apprehending Zachary Nelson?"

Dick Chalmers' flat brown eyes turned on her. "Getting close. He's in Reno."

"So what's the hold up?"

"There isn't one. We've alerted local authorities there, and we have extra agents flying in." He glanced at the clock on the far wall. "In fact, they should have landed a few minutes ago."

"And you know his exact location?"

"Yes."

"So why haven't you had the local police pick him up?"

"We'd rather keep this in-house. Some local rookie might get scared and start shooting. We don't want that, now, do we?"

"I don't know," Alana hedged. "It might not be the worst outcome."

The director's creepy eyes focused on her like he was seeing her for the first time. Several seconds ticked by as his gaze locked with hers. She waited silently.

"Ah. Good point." Suddenly he whirled, then hustled into a private booth with a secure phone.

Alana smiled. Perhaps he'd gotten her drift. It certainly looked like it.

And she hadn't had to say anything incriminating. She'd said nothing that would come back to bite her later. She'd maintained absolute, total deniability.

All while setting up this Zachary James Nelson for likely assassination.

She truly couldn't have planned it better if she'd tried.

CHAPTER ELEVEN

Katie stayed in the right lane behind the motorhome as they drove northeast toward Fernley on I-80. Her thoughts grew troubled.

Why had Evan told Zach to stay off the interstates?

Obviously he'd seen the news, that Zach was a person of interest in the California attacks.

What else had he seen or heard? Were the cops watching I-80?

Katie hadn't been catching the radio news, because they'd been so focused on avoiding getting caught. But it was close to the top of the hour now, so she turned on the radio.

"...ground zero is apparently the downtown financial district of Manhattan," the announcer said.

Katie blinked. Ground zero? Manhattan? *What?*

Where was the news about California?! And Zach?

"Officials are urging residents to take shelter in basements and underground facilities that will provide some shielding from nuclear radiation," he continued.

WHAT? Katie almost slammed on her brakes. Nuclear what?!

"It's unclear at this time if the New York attack is related to the California attack," the reporter said. "The president and her cabinet are reported to be in a secure, undisclosed location. We are still waiting for official word from the administration."

Katie grabbed her walkie talkie and turned it on. "Zach? Runner! Runner, are you there?"

"Copy that, Mermaid, go ahead."

"Turn on your radio! The news!"

Rustling and static came through the walkie speaker, and it sounded like he'd turned on his radio.

"Is it about me?" he asked.

"No! New York got nuked! At least, I think that's what happened."

He responded with a low whistle. "Whoa!"

"Crazy! I can't believe it," she said. "I mean, after yesterday...."

"Shhh, I'm listening!"

Katie hushed and turned up the pickup's radio volume. It cut to a commercial. She turned it off.

"Well, at least they're not talking about me anymore," he said.

"You mean, at the moment."

"And they're going to have a hard time pinning *that* on me. I was running for my life when that happened. And don't know the first thing about bombs!"

"Sure. Unless they think you're connected to a terror cell that did both attacks, and by catching you, they can squeeze you for information about the bomb."

She didn't say *torture*, but she shuddered when she thought it.

"Thank you. That's encouraging." His tone dripped sarcasm.

"Sorry, babe." She sighed. "I don't know what to say."

Heavier traffic and buildings ahead indicated they were approaching Fernley.

"Have you thought about what Evan said?" Katie asked. "About the interstates?"

"Yeah, but I can't make any sense of it."

"Maybe he knows something we don't," she said. "Do you think we should leave I-80?"

"There aren't a lot of other options in the Nevada desert. I mean, we're making miles now, finally. If we got off on some little goat trail –"

"He might be right, though. They're a lot less likely to be looking on the little highways, don't you think?"

"Who knows?" Zach said. "Tell you what – when we get into town, we'll pull off for a minute and check out our options. There aren't many roads, I know that much."

"Sounds good."

A minute later, he took the offramp into Fernley. On Main Street, they pulled up near a city park. Zach stayed in the motorhome while Katie walked over and climbed into the RV.

"Man!" His eyes widened. "I can't believe that about New York!"

"I know." Katie settled into the passenger seat.

"Mommy!" Timothy let himself out of his car seat and climbed into her lap. She wrapped her arms around him, then kissed the top of his head.

He turned azure blue eyes up to her. "I wanna ride with you!"

She smiled. "We'll see."

"I was going to use the map app on my phone," Zach said, "but we ditched the darn things!"

"Do we have any paper maps?" Katie opened the glove box and rifled through the contents.

"Of Nevada?" He stretched his arms. "I doubt it."

"We're so used to using the phones for everything." She closed the glove box and looked at him. "We need maps! How can you run for your life if you don't know where you're going?!"

Evan left his parents in the kitchen and walked into the living room, where Elizabeth and her dad sat on the sofa, watching the news on TV. As a commercial came on, Elizabeth picked up the remote and muted the sound. She turned her focus on him.

"Dad said you went to town."

"Yeah. We were at the grocery store when we heard."

The ambassador leaned forward. "How was everything there? Any unrest?"

"I don't know if I'd call it that. I think the ATM ran out of cash because the store and the gas station weren't taking credit cards. Or debit cards." Evan flexed his fingers. "There were lines everywhere. People couldn't find carts or parking spaces at the grocery store."

The older man nodded knowingly. "That sounds about right. It's the first phase."

Evan bit his lip. Did he want to know what the other phases were? His curiosity won out.

"What's the second phase?"

"Anger. Frustration. Fights." The ambassador glanced at his daughter, then back to Evan. "After that, all kinds of craziness. Looting, violence and chaos."

"Clear out here in the boonies?" He found it hard to imagine. "I mean, I'm glad we're not in Baltimore right now, or even D.C., but... violence in Galloway?"

"Tranquility is a fragile thing," the ambassador said.

Mom and Dad came into the living room and settled in the remaining chairs. Mom's face still looked pale.

"I can't believe all this," she said. "It's too much. All at oncc."

"What should we be doing?" Dad turned to the ambassador. "Zach and Katie are out there somewhere with our grandson. We can't reach them. Can't help them."

"If you're people of prayer, I'd recommend that right now."

Evan felt his eyebrows lift. It'd been a long time since he'd seen his parents pray. Personally, he hadn't been in a church in over a decade, other than for weddings and funerals. He was pretty sure it'd been at least that long for his parents, too.

Were they even still Christians? Was he?

Probably not. He never gave it a thought. On the other hand, of course he was! He certainly wasn't a Buddhist or a Hindu. He believed in God and Jesus, he just wasn't concerned about it.

"I was thinking more along practical lines," Dad answered. "I mean, what do you need to do when your country is under attack? How do you protect yourself? What about your assets? We can't reach Zach, but we don't want his inheritance to go up in smoke."

"He's talking about our retirement," Mom said. "Our pensions, our investments. What can we do to get ahead of the pack on this?"

Seriously! She was doing it again – they both were. Evan dropped his head to hide his embarrassment. The world could go up in flames, but they had to protect their money.

If his parents had a god, that was it. Wealth.

As Alana took calls from Bob Osgood, director of CAL-FIRE, and Thomas Abrams, the state's fire marshal, her mind kept drifting to the FBI's manhunt for Zachary James Nelson.

Would law enforcement officers take him alive?

Or would they "accidentally" kill him during his arrest?

She was setting up an innocent man. Why didn't she feel bad about that?

"Madam Vice President?" Mr. Abrams said. "Did that make sense?"

Alana forced her thoughts back to the conversation, only part of which she'd missed.

"Right. Yes. So you've been able to protect a few neighborhoods, where the wind was favorable."

"Very few, I'm afraid. But there were also some smaller communities that were not hit by the fires."

"That's good."

"They're cut off at this point, though. No food, water service or electricity, and residents can't evacuate because either they're surrounded by fires, or the freeways are impassible."

"Still?" Alana wondered. "I mean, what's the current status of the interstates?"

"Totally clogged. Lots of people got tired of waiting, and abandoned their cars. Or they ran out of gas." The fire marshal sighed. "I guess after the fires are put out, the government will have to remove all those vehicles. Millions of them. It could take months just to open I-5."

Alana scowled.

Man! California had gone from biggest state economy to total wasteland overnight.

Her thoughts skittered to New York, then to the fall guy. Ugh! It was so hard to focus on just one problem.

"Is Mexico keeping its border crossings open?"

"Yes, but very little traffic is getting there now. The roads are blocked by abandoned vehicles about ten miles from the border. Lots of people who were that close ended up walking after they ran out of gas on the highway. So basically, it's down to a trickle of evacuees on foot today."

Alana pressed her fingers against her forehead, then released a heavy sigh. "It's just... unbelievable."

"And the thing in New York," Mr. Abrams said. "I mean – this is so crazy!"

"I know. I can't believe it." She cussed under her breath.

"Well, when you catch that Zachary Nelson guy, I want to personally be there when you fry him," he said. "Give the freak a little taste of his own medicine!"

"I'll send you an engraved invitation," Alana promised.

She ended the call and leaned back in her chair.

Hopefully, it'd never get that far. If all went well, Mr. Nelson would be dead by the end of the day.

Which was wrong, because he was innocent – but this way was best for the country. The United States needed closure on the terrorist attack in California, and Mr. Nelson would deliver that.

Wasn't it better to let one innocent man take the blame and punishment, rather than allow the Muslims to bear the stigma because one extremist Muslim had decimated the state?

Of course it was!

She kneaded her neck muscles. In reality, it hadn't been just one Muslim. A whole terrorist network of them, numbering at least in the hundreds, had torched California.

Then there were the ones who'd flown the drones at airports.

All of these people were still out there, running loose.

Nobody was looking for them.

They were only looking for the blogging pastor, who actually wasn't involved at all.

Well, perhaps the government was looking for the airport drone operators, but those guys had only taken down seven airliners. Small potatoes, given all the other stuff going on.

Like the attack on New York. Who'd done that?

In all probability, given the time frame, it was a major terrorist network that had launched all these attacks on the United States. Perhaps funded by a rogue Islamic country.

How many more attacks did they have planned?

How many more could the country withstand?

Alana glanced around the PEOC as her colleagues focused on their investigations. Would the government ever try to find and prosecute the people who were actually doing all this?

CHAPTER TWELVE

"We're going to have to buy some maps," Katie said. "Maybe a gas station will have some."

"Or a visitor center." Zach rubbed his eyes. "I didn't get near enough sleep last night."

Katie boosted Timothy off her lap.

"I really don't like going into stores." She frowned. "Somebody is going to recognize me from all the pictures on TV and the internet."

"Maybe we could send Timothy." Zach caught her gaze and winked.

She almost laughed.

"In ten years!" She opened the door and slid out. "Let me borrow your hat."

Zach handed her one of his baseball caps, and she put it on.

"You look cute. Keep it low, and try to avoid security cameras."

"That's the plan. I'll be back in a few minutes, if I don't get caught."

His brow wrinkled. "I'll be praying until you get back."

"Thanks." She closed the door, returned to the pickup, and drove down the street to a gas station.

It'd be best if she could slip in while they were busy, but there was only one vehicle at the gas pumps, and one other one in front of the building.

A slow day. Great.

She sent up a prayer, pulled down the brim of her hat, and hurried to the door, head low.

Stepping inside, she scanned the store. To her left, a young guy in an orange t-shirt ran the checkout counter. To the right stood aisles of junk food. Refrigerator cases of cold drinks lined the side walls and the back, and signs for restrooms were posted near the ceiling in the far corner.

She approached the cashier.

"Do you have maps?"

He raised his eyebrows. "Are you serious? Nobody uses maps anymore."

"So you don't have any?"

He pointed toward the corner near the restrooms. "Maybe there's some trucker atlases back there."

She hurried over and found a stack of dusty atlases on a bottom shelf. Right next to a wire rack with maps. She grabbed the Nevada map, then decided to get one for Idaho, too. And Oregon.

At the front of the store, she got in line behind a slim blonde woman about her age who was paying for gas and cigarettes. She got her change, then glanced Katie's way as she turned to leave.

She turned again and looked closely at Katie.

"Don't I know you?" she asked, hazel eyes fixed on her.

"No." Katie wanted to disappear. "I'm not from here."

The woman cocked her head. "Where're you from?"

Katie stepped up to the checkout and put her maps on the counter.

"California," she answered when the woman kept staring at her.

"Well, what d'ya know? Maps!" The clerk said.

Katie pulled her wallet from her purse.

"You just look so familiar," the woman insisted.

Katie shrugged and gave the woman what she intended to be a dismissive look. "Sorry."

"That's $13.95," the clerk said.

She handed him a twenty.

"Are you a movie star? I'm sure I've seen you."

"Hardly." Katie averted her eyes. "Nope. I'm just a mom."

The clerk counted back her change. "Do you want a bag?"

"No." Katie dropped the money in her purse and dropped her wallet in after it. She grabbed the maps.

The woman stood between her and the exit.

"You must be famous. Tell me who you are!" She put her hands on her hips.

"Seriously!" Katie brushed past her. "Stop harassing me, or I'll call the cops."

She shoved the door open and escaped into the fresh air. The last thing she'd do was call the cops. But she had to get away from this nosy woman. Who'd obviously seen a photo of Katie today.

Footsteps fell behind her. The woman called her a nasty name.

Whatever. Katie hurried to the pickup and climbed in, glad to shut the door and get out of there.

The blonde got into the vehicle parked at the gas pumps.

Katie put the truck in gear, then paused. Maybe she should let the woman leave first, so she wouldn't follow Katie. Straight to Zach, whom she'd almost certainly recognize.

With heat in his cheeks, Evan stared hard at the rug as Ambassador Wilford cleared his throat.

"Financially, I'd say it's too late to do anything other than get a handful of bills from the local ATM, which you've already done. The banks aren't open because it's Sunday, and I doubt they'll open tomorrow, given the huge blow to the financial district in New York."

Evan lifted his gaze, but avoided glancing toward Elizabeth. The ambassador focused on Mom and continued.

"No, I believe any money in the system is stuck there indefinitely. Perhaps permanently."

Mom's brown creased. "Not just bank accounts... stocks, bonds... all of it?"

He nodded.

"New York City is the financial heart of the country. And somebody just stabbed a dagger in it. Obviously, the New York Stock Exchange won't be open for business. It was incinerated." He turned his blue eyes on Evan. "If any banks try to open tomorrow, it'll just be another disaster. Everybody will show up for cash, and most branches don't have more than ten to twenty thousand on hand."

Dad's face reddened. "That's ridiculous!"

"Yes, but that's the way it is," the ambassador said. "Most people don't use much cash anymore. Other than drug dealers and other criminal organizations."

He leaned back in his chair and glanced at his daughter. Evan stole a glance at Elizabeth, too. She sat erect, hands folded on her lap, legs crossed gracefully at her ankles. Elegant.

So out of his league.

Mom pressed her lips together, then wrung her hands.

"How long do you think this will last?" She asked. "I mean, I only bought about a week's worth of groceries. I hope the banks are open by Friday!"

"It's hard to say." Ambassador Wilford frowned. "It may be a very long time."

"Weeks?" Dad asked.

"Months?" Elizabeth leaned back in her chair and focused on her father. "This is it, isn't it?"

He nodded, looking only at her. "I believe so, yes."

"This is what?" Mom asked. "I can't believe the banks would be closed for months!"

A sick feeling weighted Evan in his seat. What was Elizabeth talking about? He leaned forward, almost holding his breath, as the ambassador began to explain.

"This may very well be the collapse of America," he said. "From which our nation never recovers."

Dad waved his hand dismissively. "Come on! We're the wealthiest, strongest country in the world! We weathered 9/11, and we'll weather this."

That was right. Evan drew in a deep breath and tried to relax his shoulders. The United States had bounced back from everything so far – civil war, two world wars, terrorist attacks – this was just one more crisis she'd endure. Wasn't it?

"This is different," the ambassador said. "If this is our actual fall, it will be permanent. I believe according to prophecy, our nation will be destroyed very swiftly, and that will be the end of us."

He stopped there, as if uncertain whether anyone wanted to hear more. Well, Evan did, for one!

"Please, go on," he urged.

The old man looked at him, focusing those blue eyes like lasers on Evan.

"There are prophecies in the scriptures that we believe describe the United States and her final destruction, not too long before other end times events," he said. "They indicate that the U.S. reneges on a promise to defend Israel from her attackers, and is punished by swift and permanent demolition."

This was news to Evan. True, he didn't attend church any more, but he didn't recall hearing anything like this when he did go to church as a child, either.

"I thought we're supposed to be raptured," Mom said. "Before anything bad happens."

"No, but that's a separate discussion," Ambassador Wilford said. "In any case, the destruction of America occurs before the tribulation, if my understanding is correct."

Evan's heart thumped in his chest.

If their guest was correct, and the country was being destroyed right now – well, it was almost too much to comprehend. The human death toll and the suffering would be incalculable.

Where could one go to hide from such devastation?

Alana cornered the FBI director.

"I need an update on our manhunt."

"They were in Reno," Director Chalmers said. "Our license plate scanners caught Mr. Nelson entering the city, and we pinged his phone there."

She narrowed her eyes. "I thought you knew exactly where he was! Reno isn't a small place."

He shrugged and fixed his soulless brown eyes on hers.

"We'll get him. If he leaves town, the license scanners will alert us. If he gets gas, we'll know. If he gets a room, we'll know."

She felt heat rising in her neck.

"Why can't you just ping his phone again? That will tell us exactly where he is right now!"

"We've been trying, but it's not responding. He may have destroyed it, or his batteries died. With any luck, he'll put it on a charger, and we'll be ready to pounce."

Alana touched the base of her throat.

"He might get away." She spoke quietly, her gaze moving around the PEOC, settling on Basilia.

“Not a chance,” the director scoffed. “We’ll have him in an hour. You’ll see.”

Her eyes snapped toward his face.

“How many times have you said that? And how many hours has it already been?!”

Raising himself to his full height, he squared his shoulders and spoke quietly.

“As you well know, many of our resources have suddenly been diverted to focus on the eastern side of the country. But the FBI is resourceful and well equipped. We’ll get your guy. And we’ll figure out who attacked New York.”

He paused and stared at her. “A little patience would be appreciated.”

“I’m afraid I’m all out of that.” Alana leaned toward him. “I need this guy off the streets.”

“We’ll take care of it.”

“You’d better. And you know why.”

Dick Chalmers knew just as well as she did why Zachary James Nelson needed to be reeled in ASAP. Their fall guy needed to be silenced.

CHAPTER THIRTEEN

After the nosy blonde woman left the gas station parking lot, Katie returned to the city park where Zach was waiting. But she didn't pull up near him, she parked around the corner. Just in case that lady realized who Katie was, and decided to look for her or call the cops. She knew what Katie was driving. And since this was a tiny town, it'd take the authorities all of thirty seconds to find the pickup.

Grabbing the maps, she hurried to the motorhome and climbed into the passenger seat.

"I'm hungry, Mama!"

She glanced back and saw Timothy patting Duke.

"Just a minute, Tim." She handed the maps to Zach. "I almost got made by a woman at the gas station. We need to get out of here quick."

He opened the Nevada map. "I was praying like a preacher the whole time you were gone."

"God was listening. That lady was tenacious, let me tell you!" She climbed back into the main compartment of the motorhome. "I'm going to make some PBJ sandwiches. Tim can have his now, and we can eat while we drive."

"Don't use too much jelly, or the little man and I will have some sticky messes."

"I'll use bananas, instead."

"Perfect."

As Zach pored over the map, Katie whipped up the sandwiches, buckled Timothy back in his car seat at the dinette, and gave him two halves.

"What do you say?" She prompted.

"Thank you, Mama! Thank you, Jesus!"

"Amen." Katie took the other sandwiches up front and settled in the passenger seat. "Okay, what'd you find out?"

"Basically, we can take Hwy. 50 south, or continue northeast on I-80 to Winnemucca." He held the map so she could see it. "There's also this little state route, 447, that runs north and eventually cuts into the northeast corner of California. It looks like you can continue on to Oregon that way."

"That sounds good." Katie took a bite of her sandwich.

"I don't know... it's a tiny road out in the middle of nowhere. And it might be cut off by fires at some point," Zach said.

"But it'd definitely get us off the beaten path. I mean, who'd look for us up there?"

"There doesn't appear to be any towns or anything."

Katie glanced out the window at passing traffic. "Sounds good to me."

"Not if we can't even get gas. Or if we get caught in a wildfire."

She sighed. "Fine. I just want to get out of here. Where do you want to go?"

"I think we should head up to Winnemucca."

"Your brother said we should stay off the interstates. That was the whole reason we stopped here in Fernley to get maps in the first place!" She couldn't keep the frustration out of her tone.

"We needed the maps because we don't have our phones anymore."

"Whatever." She watched a city police car cruise past. Her heart sped up. "Let's just get out of this town."

As soon as the coast was clear, she got out of the RV.

"I'll follow you." She closed the door and hurried back to the pickup, looking over her shoulder several times.

Everything around the park appeared peaceful, but she knew that could all change in a single second.

Evan leaned forward in his seat, fastening his gaze on Ambassador Wilford.

"Could you explain a little more?" He asked. "About the prophecy?"

"Of course." The white-haired gentleman placed his coffee cup on the end table between him and his daughter.

"The scriptures describe a massive attack on Israel in the end times, in which God himself rescues the tiny nation by bringing nature's forces to bear against her invaders. I believe we witnessed that in April."

"The Russian invasion," Mom said.

"Right," he agreed. "Also known prophetically as the first Gog-Magog War."

"Gog-Magog?" She tilted her head. "What's that?"

"Magog is Russia, and Gog was the leader of the coalition. I'm not certain if Gog refers to the Russian president in person, or the spiritual entity who possesses him. In any case, the April war played out according to prophecies in Ezekiel."

"But that war involved a lot more countries than just Russia," Dad objected.

"Yes, and the Old Testament prophecies included other countries as well. Iran, eastern Europe, northern Africa –"

"That was all spelled out in the Bible?" Evan interrupted. "I mean, seriously... why haven't we heard this until just now?"

A knowing smile crossed the ambassador's face. "You think the leaders of godless media outlets and pagan countries, like ours have become, want to point people to the Bible?"

"But if it's true..." Evan stopped. What if it was true? If no one ever learned the truth? If it was buried forever by people who opposed it?

He looked across at the ambassador, who was looking intently at him.

"Here's the other thing," Ambassador Wilford said. "Prophecy often has to be interpreted. For example, the prophets three or four thousand years ago did not use our modern nations' names. Ezekiel spoke of Magog, not Russia. Of Gomer and Tubal and Put and Cush. Likewise, the United States is not named, but we're in there, too."

"How?" Mom asked. "How can you know we're in there? That there's any reference to us?"

Somehow, the conversation had taken a wild turn from a discussion on protecting their assets to interpreting old prophecies. But Evan found himself intrigued by it all.

Because if the Bible foretold the April war, and it foretold the imminent destruction of the United States, what else might be in there?

And what should he do about it?

Zach knew all this stuff, surely. He and Katie were diehard Christians. Why hadn't Zach told him? Or if he had, why hadn't Evan listened?

He scooted forward in his seat.

He was ready to listen now!

An FBI aide approached Director Chalmers, and Alana took a step closer. The president had put her in charge of collating intel related to the California attack, and she didn't want to miss a single update. The aide glanced at her before speaking to the director.

"We have reason to suspect Mr. Nelson has left Reno," he said.

A grimace creased Dick Chalmers' face momentarily. "Go on."

"We've had agents personally review all the surveillance footage on routes out of the city. They've spotted a vehicle that they think might be Mr. Nelson's."

"They think? Can't they see the license plate?" The director crossed his arms.

"No, sir. That's the problem. The vehicle was directly behind a semi when it traveled past the cameras, and the cameras only record on-coming traffic."

Alana felt like yelling, but she managed to rein in her anger. "You're saying it didn't register on the license scanners?"

"Exactly." The aide clicked a pen he was holding.

"How can this happen?" Her hands curled into fists. "I thought those scanners recorded every single plate!"

The FBI director turned to face her like he was addressing a child. "Ninety-nine percent of the time, they do. Once in a while, like in this case, where the vehicle might be tucked in behind a larger truck, they miss a plate."

Alana couldn't believe it. She closed her eyes. When she spoke, her words were clipped.

"So. Where is he now?"

"If our agents are correct, he's on Interstate 80."

"Going where?" she asked.

"East, towards Winnemucca."

She glared at the director with a pointed expression. "Now what?"

"We'll maintain surveillance in Reno, in case the agents made a mistake. And we'll alert local authorities east of Reno and in the Winnemucca area." He folded his arms and focused on his aide. "Also, we'll relocate staff to Winnemucca by air."

"Yes, sir." With his new marching orders, the aide scurried away.

Alana couldn't look at the FBI director. She wanted to claw his creepy eyes out.

CHAPTER FOURTEEN

Katie followed Zach out of Fernley, back onto I-80. Something about this didn't feel right. The freeway made her nervous. She watched the traffic around her, and in her mirrors, almost expecting to see flashing lights.

Were they doing the wrong thing? Should they have taken one of the little highways out of town?

She thought so.

Had they prayed for guidance on this choice?

Nope. Zach had just picked Winnemucca.

And that's where they were headed now, come what may. Once on I-80 east of Fernley, they really didn't have any other choice. For the next two hours, they were going to be traveling this highway.

Sure, they could make a stop mid-way, at Lovelock, but then they'd just have to board the interstate again. There weren't any other routes out of Lovelock.

She ran her fingers through her hair. It hadn't been washed since Friday morning, and could use a good shampoo.

Slowly, she expelled a deep breath. Glanced again in her rearview mirror.

Everything looked normal, but she couldn't shake the growing feeling of dread snaking its way around her mind.

They should have stayed off the interstate. Like Zach's brother said.

But there was nothing she could do about it now.

Just drive.

And pray.

She looked up into the blue sky.

I'm sorry, Lord. I think we made the wrong choice. Would you please cover us? And help us to remember to ask for your guidance next time.

As the Nevada desert rolled out in front of her, Katie relaxed her tense muscles.

They were in God's hands now.

"Would anyone like some tea or coffee?" Mom rose from her chair.

Ambassador Wilford and his daughter declined, and so did Evan.

"I'll have some coffee," Dad said. "But you stay here. I'll go get it."

He went to the kitchen, and Mom sat back down.

"This is really interesting." She looked from the ambassador to Elizabeth. "I hope you two can stay for a little while. Are we keeping you from other plans?"

"I think we could stay a little longer." A sweet smile lit Elizabeth's face. She looked to her father. "Unless you need to go."

"And do what? The president won't see me, and the vice president won't listen!" He tossed his hands in the air, then winked at her. "At least here, I have a captive audience."

"They won't listen?" Evan was taken aback. "Why not? I mean

– you know all this stuff about events that are taking place right now! Huge, major events."

The ambassador shrugged his thin shoulders and adjusted his bifocals.

"I suspect they see me as the last vestige of an old, white, patriarchal generation of has-beens." He sighed. "I'm sure they're already making a list of candidates to take my place."

He reached over and put his hand on his daughter's. "It's just as well, anyway. I've done what I could. Time to retire."

Dad returned from the kitchen with his coffee. "What's this about retirement?"

"Dad's going to throw in the towel," Elizabeth announced.

"Really?" Dad sat on the sofa. "When?"

"Oh, soon, I guess." The ambassador smiled. "Perhaps tomorrow."

"What? Seriously?" Evan's gaze jumped to their guest. "Is it because of the attacks?"

"It's because of the prophecy," Ambassador Wilford clarified. "I expect there won't be much need for a U.S. ambassador to Israel in the future."

"Because you think there won't be much of a U.S." Mom frowned. "Based on the scriptures."

"That pretty much sums it up," he agreed.

"How do you know those prophecies refer to the United States?"

"Good question. Since the prophets didn't use that name, obviously." The ambassador leaned back, looking very much like a professor of philosophy. Or ancient antiquities. "The prophets gave clues to identify the nation that betrays Israel and is destroyed for that betrayal."

"Such as?" Evan felt like he had to drag each morsel of information from this guy.

"I'll just give you a few for now," he said. "First, this Daughter of Babylon, as Jeremiah calls her, is also referred to in Revelation as Babylon the Great and a mystery. This country is called, 'the hammer of the whole earth.'"

His gaze roved from Evan to Mom. "Can you imagine any other nation in the world today being referred to as the hammer of the whole earth?"

Mom shook her head. "But at different times in history, it could have referred to other countries."

"Right! Except that this mystery Babylon the Great betrays Israel in the latter days. At the end of the world. So it couldn't have been any previous point in history."

"Okay," Mom said. "What else?"

"This country is the hindermost, or last, of the nations of the world. Now, Europe and the Middle East, Africa and Asia – they all have cities that have been populated for thousands of years. The United States?"

He spread his hands to make his point. "We're a very young country, in the scheme of things."

"That's pretty vague, though," Dad said. "Is there anything more specific?"

"Oh, there's lots!"

Evan sat up straight. This was going to get good.

"It's a nation of great wealth and luxury," the ambassador said. "It's a multi-ethnic, multi-cultural country. It sits on many waters – and the United States sits on the Pacific and Atlantic and Arctic Oceans. We've got the Great Lakes and the Mississippi and the Columbia and –"

"Got it. Lots of water," Dad agreed. "What else?"

"It's the center of world commerce," he answered. "Or it was. Until today."

Alana drummed her fingers on the table. At the far end of the PEOC, the president was conversing with the CIA director. It'd be good to hear the latest on New York, but she wasn't excited about updating Basilia on the manhunt debacle.

Perhaps she could put it off until she had better news to report. How long might that be? An hour? Two?

Basilia would corner her long before then.

She might as well get it over now.

Slowly, she rose from her chair and started toward the president. The CIA director was still talking.

"...some indication the Iranians might be involved," he said, glancing toward Alana as she approached. "We have numerous leads we're following up."

Basilia's gaze shifted to Alana. "Tell me some good news."

"We don't have any yet," she admitted. "Zachary Nelson was in Reno, but the FBI believes he's on his way to Winnemucca. His phone isn't pinging, and apparently he's not using his credit cards."

"Nobody's using credit cards," the president said. "Major banks are obliterated, servers are down, and the few places that maybe could take them are refusing to."

That made sense, given the situation in New York that Alana hadn't had any updates on.

"Why can't they ping his phone?" Basilia pressed.

"Either the battery died, or he destroyed it."

"I'm sure by now he knows we're after him." The president turned back to the CIA director. "You were saying you think the Iranians nuked us?

"It's too early to be sure, but some of our intel points that way," he said.

Basilia cussed.

"I need facts!" She waved him away like a fly. "Go! Find some!"

As he retreated, the president turned her attention to the FBI director. She snapped her fingers.

"Have you picked up Ambassador Wilford yet?"

"We've knocked at his apartment. He doesn't appear to be home."

She scowled. "What do you mean, doesn't appear to be? Didn't you go in and check?"

"We were tempted to, but we didn't have a warrant. In any case, his vehicle is gone and his phone isn't there either."

"Where's his phone?" She glanced at Alana and rolled her eyes.

"We pinged it in some little Appalachian community. Galloway, West Virginia."

"He's hiding out!" The president pointed her finger at Dick Chalmers' chest. "Go get him!"

CHAPTER FIFTEEN

An uneventful hour passed, and Katie began to see signs for Lovelock. If only they could get off the freeway here and take another highway! But according to the maps, the only way into and out of the city was on the interstate. They had about another hour to Winnemucca, where she'd urge Zach to take another road. In fact, she'd insist on it.

Her spirit wasn't liking this place. Maybe they should just get out of Nevada at the first opportunity.

As the approached the Lovelock exit, Zach signaled to leave the highway.

Her radio squawked at the same time. "Mermaid? You there?"

"Go ahead, Runner. What's going on?"

"Little man needs a potty break."

"He can do that while you're driving," she said. Timothy was old enough now to get out of his car seat and use the bathroom while the RV was on the road.

"Big man needs one, too."

She chuckled. "Fine. Let's make it quick, though."

He exited the freeway and drove into town, with Katie right

behind him. Not finding a better location, he just parked on the side of the street.

She was ready to stretch her legs. Donning sunglasses and a hat, she hopped out of the pickup and hurried up to the motorhome. Duke greeted her at the door.

Zach was retrieving a root beer from the fridge. He held one out toward her.

"Want one?"

She waved it off. "Nah, I'm good."

The toilet flushed, and Timothy came out of the bathroom. He looked from one parent to the other. "Want one what?"

Katie laughed and mussed his blond mop. "Did you wash your hands?"

He nodded.

"I'm not sure. Go wash them again."

He dropped his head and went back into the bathroom. Water ran in the sink.

Katie turned to Zach.

"I'm really uncomfortable being on the interstate."

He nodded. "I know. We'll get off in Winnemucca. Until then, we're kind of stuck."

"Trapped," she said.

He eyed her. "You think it's that bad?"

"Over two hours on one inescapable freeway?" She paused. "Oh, yeah."

Timothy returned to the kitchen and watched his dad take a gulp of pop. "Can I have some?"

"You can have the rest, buddy." Zach handed off the can, which Katie guessed was nearly empty already. He went into the bathroom.

"Come on, let's get you buckled in." Katie took the pop and set it on the dinette table while she buckled the little guy into his car seat on the bench.

Moments later, Zach returned. "Ready to roll?"

"I think I'll use the room, too," she answered. "Then I'll be ready."

After using the bathroom, Katie put her sunglasses back on.

"Should we fill the tanks here, or wait until Winnemucca?" she asked.

"I'm only down a quarter," Zach said. "I think we can wait."

That sounded good. They'd probably have around half a tank when they got to Winnemucca, which was plenty.

"Sounds good. Let's hit the road!"

A few minutes later, they took the onramp to I-80 east. In about an hour, they'd be able to get off the freeway.

As far as she was concerned, it couldn't happen too soon.

Evan's mind whirled. This was amazing information. It was like the ambassador was describing the United States, right from the ancient manuscripts, centuries before the country was envisioned or conceived.

By anyone other than God, anyway.

"Please, go on," he urged.

"Sure," Ambassador Wilford scratched his forehead. "Let's see... the Daughter of Babylon is where the nations gather."

He glanced around the room. "United Nations, anyone? In New York City?"

"Destroyed today," Dad said.

"Exactly!" The ambassador nodded. "Jeremiah 51 says that nations will not flow to the Daughter of Babylon anymore. Maybe they'll relocate to Brussels or somewhere else in Europe."

"But that does seem to indicate the United States," Mom said. "The nations have gathered here for years. In more ways than one – like immigration, they all flow here!"

"Yes. And Jeremiah also says this country has been proud against the Lord. Other verses indicate this Daughter of Babylon has a significant Jewish population. The vast majority of all the Jews in the world live either in the United States or Israel. And the state with the most Jews in it? New York!"

"Wow," Evan said. "I didn't realize that."

"Also, the Daughter of Babylon is a nation of deep water ports. The shipping merchants all became wealthy because of her."

Dad touched his chest. He looked at Mom. "This definitely sounds more and more like America."

"Absolutely," the ambassador agreed. "There are more clues, too. But you can already see it is most likely us. The hammer of the whole earth."

"So now what?" Evan asked, almost afraid to hear the answer, but needing to know it anyway. It was like being tested for cancer, and waiting for the results. You had to know what was going to happen to you.

Mom wrapped her hands around her knee.

"Yes, what does the prophecy say will happen to us?" She asked.

Ambassador Wilford looked ominously from one to the other.

"The Daughter of Babylon will be destroyed. Very rapidly. Some verses indicate in a single day –"

"Like California!" Evan interrupted.

The ambassador nodded. "Other verses say in an hour."

"Like a nuclear bomb in New York." Mom frowned. "This isn't looking good. Is there a possibility of... recovery? Rebuilding?"

"Not according to the scriptures." He sighed. "They say merchants on ships will back off, for fear of her torment, while watching her burn."

"I'm sure that's happening in California right now," Mom said.

"Not to mention New York," Dad added. "Nobody wants to get downwind of all that radioactive fallout."

"Exactly," the ambassador agreed. "And I think a nuclear attack was indicated by scriptures, given that description, and that afterwards, no one would live there anymore."

"Maybe the Daughter of Babylon is just New York City," Evan suggested. "I mean, they were the place that got nuked. Not the whole country."

"I've wondered that myself," Ambassador Wilford agreed. "But the Daughter of Babylon is supposed to be punished for betraying Israel when she was attacked. It wasn't New York City that betrayed her, it was the United States as a nation."

He pressed his hands together. "In any case, even with just a single strike on that city, our entire country will be plunged into chaos. We're about to witness a financial collapse of unprecedented proportions. The end result will be the same – America will be thrown off the world stage, just as the end times get under way. Which explains why there's no mention of us in the prophecies about the tribulation period. If we weren't destroyed, you would think we'd play a significant role in the world at that time, since we're the world's only superpower."

"Or we were." Evan's voice was hoarse. "Until this weekend."

Alana almost felt bad for the FBI director. She kept hounding him about the manhunt for Zachary Nelson, while the president had him chasing after the ambassador to Israel. He was also overseeing his agency's investigation of the terrorist attacks – although he'd pulled them off finding the actual California attackers and directed them to go after the fall guy.

But she didn't feel too bad for Director Chalmers.

This was his job, after all. He'd signed up for it.

Although he could have had no way of knowing something like this would occur during his tenure.

She eased into her chair and picked up the remote control, clicking on the television installed on the wall opposite her. Reducing the volume so it wouldn't bother those working around the table, she clicked through the channels.

The images coming out of New York now were gripping.

The media replayed clip after clip of the mushroom cloud over Manhattan, interspersed with people running away from the blast zone.

In what Alana imagined would become iconic footage of the event, a young, dark-haired mother ran up the sidewalk straight toward the camera, her left hand gripping her little boy's arm, and her right hand clutching a baby girl to her chest. The mushroom cloud loomed behind her, over her shoulder.

Moments before she would have run past the videographer, the woman tripped on the sidewalk and sprawled onto the concrete, her son tumbling with her, her daughter pressed to her side.

The woman rose with bloodied knees, smoothing the baby's hair as she squalled. Then the lady grabbed her son's hand and resumed running.

Alana's stomach turned.

They'd never make it. Tomorrow, all three would likely be dead. Or the day after, at least. They were too close to the blast zone. Same with the poor fool videoing them. Radiation sickness would claim them all.

Unable to watch more of that, she changed the channel.

Coverage of California played out on the screen. The smoke rose from Los Angeles like a bombed out war zone. How were they getting those images? Helicopter? Drone?

It was almost astonishing that journalists and photographers were still working in California.

Why weren't they running for their lives?

Had their corporate media bosses promised them safe evacuation if they'd stay on the job a few more hours or days?

If they had, they were liars. Nobody had safe routes out of that state. Motionless vehicles clogged the highways, fires devoured the now-closed airports, and walking was a long shot at best. In a day or two, California would be looking a lot like

Venezuela – no food, no water, no power – and charred to a crisp.

An ironic thought twisted Alana's lips. Well, yeah, media bosses were liars. That's what they did for a living, wasn't it? And apparently, it was what she did, as well.

After all, she was the one spinning the tale that Zachary Nelson had masterminded the California attack, when the whole cabinet knew it had been organized by none other than the governor's son.

If news of this ever got out to the American people – she shuddered.

But the news would never get out, would it?

The only people who knew the truth were the ones with her right now in the PEOC. And none of them would ever breathe a word about it.

CHAPTER SIXTEEN

After another hour on the road, signs began appearing for Winnemucca businesses. Finally. Katie couldn't wait to get off this interstate.

They approached the outskirts of town, and Zach took the first exit. It was marked for Hwy. 95, but it looked like it would take them straight into the heart of town. Moments later, they came to a big box store, and the motorhome lumbered into the parking lot, with Katie on its tail.

She sighed in relief.

Off the freeway. For some reason, it just felt better.

She climbed out of the pickup and walked to the motorhome, where she got into the passenger seat. Zach had the Nevada map spread across his lap, and the Idaho one mashed up on the dashboard.

"Where do you want to go?" he asked.

"Anywhere except back on the freeway," she said. "What are our options?"

"Extremely limited." He held the map out for her.

"We're right here," he said, pointing at northern Nevada. "We can either take U.S. 95 north into Oregon and Idaho, or we get back on I-80 and stay on it for a few hundred more miles, into Utah."

"Absolutely not!" Katie shook her head. "That's it? Only two choices?"

"Well, there's this little tiny backwater road, State Route 49, that runs through the desert back to California."

"We definitely don't want to do that," Katie said.

"So, Highway 95, then." Zach began folding the maps.

Katie glanced toward the front doors of the store. "I wonder if we should stock up on stuff here. And I was thinking about getting some hair dye."

"Are you serious? You're going to change your hair?"

"I was thinking you should, too." She glanced back toward their son, and lowered her voice. "Are we running for our lives, or what?"

"Yeah, apparently." He swallowed. "But changing our hair?"

"It's one of our most identifying characteristics," she insisted. "If you weren't blonde and I wasn't brunette –"

"What're you thinking? Redheads?" He started to smile but didn't quite get there.

"Two redheads might draw too much attention." She studied him. Couldn't quite imagine him with anything other than blond locks. "Maybe brown for you, and auburn for me?"

He sighed.

"Fine. Go ahead."

She put on her hat and pulled the brim down low. "I'll be back in ten minutes. Maybe you could study those maps and get familiar with all our options once we get on the highway going north."

"I'll do it." He gave her a serious look. "Keep your eyes open. If anything feels weird, get out of there."

"Yep." She slid out of the seat and closed the door.

If anything feels weird?

Everything felt weird. Everything *was* weird. It was difficult to imagine anything feeling weirder than it did right now, but she knew it could.

Maybe they should just hit the road. Forget about the hair dye. Just get out of this place.

Her lungs tightened as she walked toward the store. She slowly drew a deep breath and tried to release the tension in her chest and shoulders.

She was going into a store with dozens or hundreds of people in it. What if someone recognized her?

What if security stopped her?

She glanced back toward the motorhome, where her husband and son waited. Would Zach laugh at her if she panicked and came back without buying anything?

Or was entering the store a really bad idea?

A knock on the front door startled Evan.

"I'll be right back." His father rose and left the living room.

Ambassador Wilford also stood up. "Sounds like you've got visitors. And we've taken too much of your time."

"We aren't expecting anyone," Mom said. "You don't need to leave."

He checked his cell phone, then set it on the bookcase near his chair.

"I'm sure your family –" Heated words from the front porch made him pause. He turned to Evan. "It sounds like the media have found you."

"Excuse me." Evan scrambled out of his chair and hurried to the door, which was blocked by his father's body.

Beyond him, several people he didn't recognize stood on the porch, trying to peer past Dad.

"Get out of here," Dad hissed. "All of you! This is private property!"

A camera flash blinded Evan.

"Is he here?" A reporter demanded. "Is Zachary Nelson here?"

"That's it!" Dad yelled. "I'm calling the cops! You better be off my property before they get here!"

Another flash. Accompanied by half a dozen questions, all asked at once.

Several, but not all, of the media creeps retreated off the porch. Evan reached for his cell phone. Dad shut the door.

"Should I call 911?" Evan asked.

"Might as well." He twisted the deadbolt.

But Evan's call didn't go through. He followed his father back to the living room.

"The circuits are busy. Again."

"No big surprise there," the ambassador said. He looked to his daughter. "We should probably get going."

"Of course." Elizabeth rose gracefully and smiled at Evan's parents, then at him. "I'm sorry for all your trouble. Please let us know if we can do anything."

"Can you shoot reporters?" Dad asked, only half joking.

"Maybe if they break into your house." She looped her arm through her father's. "Shall we?"

He nodded and they started for the door. Reaching it, he stopped and turned back. "If I come up with anything that will help Zach, I'll let you know."

"We'd appreciate it," Mom said.

Dad unlocked the door and let them out. Evan followed them all onto the porch. The media appeared to be swarming at the end of their driveway.

Jackals!

After the ambassador and Elizabeth left, Evan followed his parents back into their cabin.

"What are we going to do if the paparazzi comes back?" he asked. "It's not like we can actually call the cops."

"We've already told them to stay off our property," Dad growled. "And I've got a shotgun."

FBI Director Chalmers made his way across the PEOC toward her, and Alana rose to meet him.

"Good news on your fugitive," he said. "He triggered a license plate scanner coming into Winnemucca."

"Finally!" It'd been hours since she'd heard any good news.

"I told you we'd get him."

"What's your plan for –" She wasn't sure how to word this. What she really wanted to know was if they'd plan to take him alive, or if they were planning to take him out.

Not really something she could ask directly, in a room full of officials, if she wanted to hang onto her deniability. Which she certainly did!

The director's dull eyes looked into hers. And seemed to read her mind.

"You're asking about the rules of engagement?" He asked. "Deadly force."

She leaned closer and whispered, "That's a green light to shoot on sight?"

He nodded. "Bingo."

"Good." She exhaled a deep breath. "How soon do you think…?"

"I'd say ten minutes, tops."

Alana nodded. "The sooner, the better."

She couldn't wait for this to be over. It was so distasteful. Murderous, actually.

But she couldn't think of it like that. No, it was necessary.

For the good of the country. For closure for Californians and their friends and relatives.

Besides, it was just one guy. And a political enemy, at that.

How many people had the United States killed – in wars, foreign coups, black ops and other exercises – in the past fifty years?

A huge, incomprehensible number, for sure.

And this was just one man.

What did he matter, in the scheme of things?

He was just a pawn, swept up in events beyond his comprehension or control.

Perhaps it'd be painless.

And quick.

And very, very soon.

Across the room, the president called for attention.

"Listen up, everybody!" She waited a moment as the PEOC fell silent. "The money people want to say something."

Alana suppressed a smile. Basilia always disdained the banking experts, and more than once released a pejorative word under her breath about them. Personally, she suspected it was because many of them were Jewish and Basilia was not known to be a fan of Jews in general.

Still, money made the world go round, and now the Secretary of the Treasury had found his way to the PEOC, where he appeared flushed and sweaty.

"Go ahead, Secretary Cohen," the president said.

The portly middle-aged man dabbed his forehead with his handkerchief.

"Thank you." He glanced around at the assembled cabinet members. "As you know, the Asian markets will be opening soon. We expect trading to be brisk, with the markets suffering heavy losses."

He ran his tongue across his teeth. Gross!

"My counterparts around the world are scrambling to make determinations about their own markets."

"What sort of determinations?" Basilia asked.

"Whether to open, or how soon to do so." He lifted a glass of water and took a quick sip. “Monday is going to be a bad day, and it could get worse from there.”

“But our markets won’t open at all,” the president said. “So we won’t have that issue.”

He glanced at her, all emotion withheld from his face.

“No, of course not. Our issues are far worse.”

CHAPTER SEVENTEEN

Katie stopped about a hundred feet from the store's entrance. Her chest constricted. Was she having a panic attack?

She'd never had one.

Was this what they felt like?

She could barely breathe!

Looking over her shoulder, she saw the motorhome and pickup at the far end of the lot. What should she do?

Then she remembered her earlier prayer. And that she needed guidance.

What should I do, Lord?

Go. Now!

The words filled her mind as surely as if someone standing beside her had just spoken them.

She turned around and beelined for the RV. It seemed to take forever to reach it. Finally, she yanked open the passenger door.

Zach wasn't in the driver's seat.

Looking back, she saw him rinsing a rag in the kitchen sink.

"Zach!"

He looked toward her, a startled expression on his face. When he saw her, the look changed to fear. He dropped the rag in the sink. "What happened?"

"We need to get out of here." She tried to sound calm, for Timothy's sake.

He glanced out the windows as he moved toward the cab. "You saw something?"

"No. I just had this bad feeling. And I prayed, and –"

"Okay, let's go." He scooted into the driver's seat and turned the key. "Follow me!"

She hustled back to the pickup, feeling only a little better. Maybe she was being ridiculous, but she wasn't imagining how she felt. Or that the government was after her husband and family.

Katie followed the motorhome out of the parking lot and back onto the street marked as Highway 95. It seemed to parallel the interstate, running east/west through Winnemucca. Then there were signs marking a left-hand turn for the highway, so Katie signaled a move into the turn lane. Zach was still in the other lane.

Had he missed the sign?

Or had he seen something, and knew a good reason to not turn and follow the highway north out of town?

She could reach him on the walkie talkie, but there wasn't really time. Either he'd get in the lane in the next couple of seconds, or they'd end up going separate directions.

Maybe she could switch back to his lane and follow him.

She checked her mirrors.

No good. Traffic was jam packed in this little crossroads town. She was stuck.

And the light turned green for the left-turning traffic.

She moved alongside Zach, whose light remained red. For a fleeting moment, her eyes met his as she drove past him, pushed along by traffic, into the intersection. He shrugged and gave her a helpless look.

And for the second time in this two-day ordeal, she was separated from him. The first time, when they were trying to get gas in Sacramento yesterday, she had Timothy and Duke with her. Now, they were with Zach. She didn't know what had caused him to skip the turn.

She looked for cop cars as she also began looking for a place to pull off and wait for Zach. Or radio him.

A glance in her rearview revealed he was crossing the intersection, continuing along the same road they'd been on. Would he circle around the block and meet up with her?

She didn't see any police cars – or really, anything suspicious.

Her eyes were filling with tears, though, so maybe she was missing something. Her heart turned to Heaven again.

Oh, Lord! Please take care of us and bring us back together. And help us escape!

The ambassador hadn't been gone ten minutes before the media idiots began pounding on the cabin door again. Evan launched out of his chair and started toward the door to tell them off.

"I was serious about that shotgun," Dad threatened.

"Hold on, Jim." Mom reached for his arm. "Let Evan get rid of them."

Evan strode to the door, unlocked it, and yanked it open, yelling, "Get the –"

The words stuck in his throat.

There were no paparazzi on the porch. Instead, a whole phalanx of FBI agents tensed like cougars ready to pounce.

In black shirts emblazoned with the Bureau logo, several of them had drawn their weapons as he'd blasted through the door, shouting. Most looked almost as surprised as he felt.

His bravado deflated like a popped balloon.

They must be here for Zach. Who, fortunately, wasn't in this part of the country. Immediately, Evan's mind went into defensive mode. Family first!

One of the agents stepped forward, holding out his badge.

"We need to speak to Ambassador Wilford," he said, looking past Evan's shoulder.

What? Not Zach?

Before he could reply, Dad answered from behind him. "You got the wrong house!"

"Can we come in?" the agent asked.

Dad stepped up beside Evan. "I just said, you have the wrong place."

His takeover of the interaction gave Evan the moment he needed to collect his wits. If these goons were after the ambassador, he'd try to protect or warn him. And he was pretty sure his parents would, too.

The first agent glanced over his shoulder at one of the other agents. Turning back to Dad, he removed his sunglasses, revealing ice blue eyes.

"We know he's here. Why are you hiding him?"

"He's not here!" Mom's voice came from just behind Evan's elbow. "Did he do something wrong?"

"We need to talk to him. We know he's here," the agent insisted.

Dad crossed his arms. "For the last time, you got the wrong house!"

Yep. His parents were circling the wagons.

The agents at the far edge of the group began whispering among themselves. What were they talking about? Were they planning to storm into the house? Arrest them all?

But since the ambassador wasn't actually in their house, it wouldn't hurt to let the goons take a look, would it?

Evan turned to his parents. "Maybe you should let them in to look around. Then they can leave."

Dad's face flamed red. "If they've got a warrant, they can look. I already told them this is the wrong place!"

This wasn't going to end well. Evan turned to the agents, trying to broker peace.

"You really do have the wrong house," he said. "And we are the only ones here. I swear!"

Alana stirred a packet of sugar into her coffee as Treasury Secretary Cohen continued his spiel.

"After the September 11th attacks, our markets were closed until September 17th. When they opened, they plummeted. The first day, we saw the largest single-day decline in the history of the New York Stock Exchange. At the end of the week, we closed the books on the worst trading week ever."

"And this will be worse," Basilia said.

"Yes, of course." He sipped his water. "We don't know when we'll be able to re-open our markets. Last time, the World Trade Center was destroyed. This time, it's the entire financial district, including the stock exchanges."

"When you say you don't know when, are you thinking weeks?" Basilia asked. "Or months?"

An irritated look flitted across his face.

"Weeks, at least, for our smaller exchanges. The U.S. has thirteen altogether."

"And the big ones?" She pressed.

"The two largest stock markets in the world are located in New York. Perhaps NASDAQ will be able to re-open elsewhere in a month or so, because all its trades are electronic. But the biggest, the New York Stock Exchange, doesn't work that way. It operates off a floor. A physical location that just got obliterated."

"Go on." Basilia stared at the man.

"The trading data is backed up to an off-site location, of

course. But the infrastructure to accommodate these kinds of exchanges will take some time. The facilities, the bandwidth, and so on. Plus, many of the floor brokers, or specialists, are presumably dead. So new staff will be hired and trained."

His shoulders drooped as he sighed. "All this takes time."

A pained look shot across Basilia's face before she lowered her head. It almost looked like defeat, which triggered warning bells in Alana's mind. The president needed to stay strong to get through this.

To get the country through this.

Back in their college days, Basilia had confided that she relied on antidepressants to stay level. That was a long time ago, though... surely she didn't still need them now. Or did she?

Alana made a mental note to consider a gentle inquiry about this – later, of course, when things were back on an even keel.

In any case, she hadn't noticed any truly unusual or worrisome behavior. So if Basilia still needed the meds, who cared? If they worked, they worked.

"So." The president raised her head and eyed Secretary Cohen. "What now?"

"With your approval, we'll issue a notice that our markets will be temporarily closed, just as they were after 9/11."

"Of course," Basilia said. "Do it."

"And we will begin the process of relocating the markets to Chicago."

"Fine."

She didn't even ask why Chicago, or if there were other options somewhere along the East Coast. She just agreed.

Alana struggled to maintain a neutral expression. It was Basilia's decision, and she needed support, not double-guessing, from her vice president. Perhaps Chicago was the only option, or the planned contingency back-up location, or perhaps there was some other reason that the president knew about, that Alana didn't know.

"Anything else?" The president asked.

The secretary shook his head. "Not at the moment."

"Fine." She glanced around the group. "What's next?"

The Homeland Security chief cleared his throat. "I have a quick update on the solar storm."

"Go ahead."

"It's not as bad as it might have been. We are seeing some minor disruptions in communications satellites and radio broadcasts. Nothing unexpected."

"I guess we'll have to live with that."

He nodded. "And it should be back to normal tomorrow."

CHAPTER EIGHTEEN

Katie drove two blocks before she found an easily accessible parking lot – just before the I-80 overpass. As she turned in, she noticed the name on the street sign. Melarkey Street.

That was fitting. Even if it did seem to be misspelled.

Wasn't it supposed to be Malarkey?

She remembered her Irish grandparents using that word when she was a child. When they were especially upset at their annoying next-door neighbor.

Just as she pulled into a parking space and shifted into park, her walkie talkie squawked.

"Mermaid."

"I'm here," she said, relief seeping into her tense muscles. "You coming around?"

"I'm trying to. I thought I saw something where we were supposed to turn."

Her eyes scanned down the street. "I didn't see anything."

"It wasn't marked," he said. "But it really looked like... that guy we were trying to avoid."

Katie caught his drift. He was obviously choosing his words

carefully because they were on an open radio channel, but he thought he'd seen an unmarked cop car.

"Okay, I'm waiting for you," she said. "Just before the overpass. You don't need to pull in here, just drive on by and I'll pull out after you and catch up."

"Sounds good. Out."

As vehicles drove past her, Katie studied each one. Was one of them an unmarked police vehicle?

She'd never know if it was. Not even by its license plate. Detectives these days were using random vehicles with standard private license plates.

It could be a minivan, or a sports car, or some old, dusty sedan.

That's how they infiltrated drug networks – by blending in and looking convincingly like normal folks.

Her heart thumped as a grey Honda went past, its driver staring at her. He wore a black t-shirt and dark sunglasses. Was he a cop, or just a guy looking for a date?

Well, he didn't need to be looking at her! Yeah, Nevada allowed legalized prostitution, but Katie was pretty sure they were regulated to certain locations or neighborhoods – a chick in a pickup truck wasn't a working girl.

So maybe he was a cop, not a creep.

He continued up the road, though, and didn't stop.

Whew!

She focused down the street toward the traffic light where she and Zach had gotten separated. A slow parade of vehicles made their way toward her, but he wasn't with them.

Where was he? She clasped her hands together.

Lord, please let him be okay. Please help us get out of this town and far from everyone who's looking for us!

A marked patrol vehicle approached from the opposite direction. Without thinking, Katie slouched in her seat and lowered the brim of her hat.

It was a city police car, and it seemed to be slowing.

Was it going to turn? Into her parking lot? Her mouth dried.

Keep going.

The patrol car had definitely slowed.

Keep going!

Just then, the motorhome came into view, about a block away. If the officer didn't turn off, he and Zach would drive right past each other. Would he recognize Zach? He was going slow enough to, that was for sure!

Turn off, turn off the road!

The cop car's turn signal came on. He was turning into Katie's parking lot.

Dear Jesus! Help!

Evan's heart thumped as two FBI agents came around from behind the cabin, where they must have been when the rest of the team was pounding on the front door. One of the men pulled an optical apparatus off his face as he approached the group.

"Well?" the apparent team leader asked.

The apparatus guy shook his head. "There's only three live bodies. Anybody else in there would be room temperature."

"Like I said!" Dad thundered. "You've got the wrong house!"

One of the agents stepped forward and whispered something in the team leader's ear.

The leader's ice blue eyes shifted briefly off Dad to his agent. "You're sure?"

"Positive."

"But his cell phone pinged right here," the leader argued. "THIS house."

"Records show a different address. Right down the road," the other guy said. "And if he's hiding here, he must be dead, since the thermographic camera only picked up three people."

"Nobody's dead," Mom said. "Nobody's hiding here."

"If you would give us permission, we'll make a quick search and be gone," the agent said, looking past Dad to Mom.

"Jim? Let's just let them. So they'll go away," she pleaded.

Dad frowned.

"Please, Jim!" Mom begged.

"Two guys." Dad stared at the leader. "Two minutes. No destruction. Agreed?"

A long moment passed as their eyes locked.

"Fine. But you all wait outside."

"Deal." Dad stepped out, with Mom on his heels. Evan followed, not happy about any of it.

"Jeffers. With me!" The leader walked into their cabin, with another agent on his heels.

On the porch, no one spoke. Evan looked out the driveway, but couldn't see the media.

Had they left? Had the FBI removed them?

Footsteps sounded on the stairs up to the loft. Moments later, they thudded down again.

After what seemed like an hour, but was probably less than three minutes, both agents exited the cabin. The leader was holding Ambassador Wilford's cell phone, which the ambassador must have forgotten earlier when he set it on the bookshelf.

"Got the phone!" He held it high so all his men could see. "Let's go!"

"That's not yours," Evan objected. "You didn't have permission to remove anything from this residence!"

Ice eyes turned his way. "It's evidence."

It wasn't. Nor was it lawfully gathered, in his opinion.

But he had to consider whether a fight on the porch with riled up FBI agents would be worth it. And the answer was a big, fat no.

It was always better to make a solid argument in court, rather than confront hot-headed cops with guns in their hands.

So he stared down the agent, but made no response.

The goons turned and silently filed off the porch and down the driveway. They hadn't even driven in. Where had they parked?

And why on earth were they going after Ambassador Wilford on stealth mode?

Alana glanced at the clock on the wall. Had it been ten minutes since she'd spoken with the FBI director? Pretty close.

Had his agents nailed their suspect in Winnemucca?

She turned toward Director Chalmers. He was deep in conversation with the Homeland Security chief. As tempting as it was to go over and butt in, she decided to wait.

Surely he'd inform her as soon as he had news.

Her stomach growled. Nerves? Or hunger?

Perhaps both. She sipped her coffee, which had almost reached room temperature. And eyed the sandwich tray in the far corner. She should probably eat something.

She made her way to the table and picked up a plate. An assortment of dainty sandwich quarters didn't really appeal to her, but she picked one up anyway, along with a tiny pickle and a few olives.

The cookies looked good, though. She grabbed a huge chocolate chip temptation and made her way back to her seat.

Her staff had left to get some sleep, and still weren't back yet. Not that she blamed them. Jason had looked beat, and Mae's fatigue showed in her eyes, if not in her face.

Alana sighed. Eventually she'd get some rest herself. When the worst of this was over.

She took a bite of her turkey sandwich. And tasted Swiss cheese, which she despised. She set the thing back on her plate and ate the pickle to get rid of the taste.

In spite of the huge events devastating millions of Americans right now, for her, the worst of it was this distasteful business with Zachary Nelson.

Her stomach rumbled again. No doubt from the Swiss cheese.

She had misgivings about setting up an innocent man, but she couldn't afford to entertain those thoughts. For one thing, it just had to happen, to give closure to the American people. For another, Basilia had made the hard call on this, with Alana's own advice and support.

She couldn't start wavering about it now.

The decision had been made. It was the best decision. Plain and simple.

She bit into her cookie, forcing herself to focus on the distraction of the chocolate deliciousness on her tongue.

Her eyes wandered again toward the FBI director.

She took another bite of cookie.

Don't think about it. It'll all be over soon.

CHAPTER NINETEEN

As the city police officer pulled into Katie's parking lot, Zach neared and gawked at her. She shook her head at him and mouthed, "Keep going!"

Tears rushed to her eyes.

Now what?

Were they really going to be busted by a local cop in backwater Winnemucca, Nevada?

DRIVE! The word burst into her mind.

She turned the key and shifted into reverse. The cop was parking two spaces over from her. At least he hadn't blocked her in. Keeping an eye on her backup camera, she eased out of her spot.

The officer climbed out of his vehicle.

Katie swung the pickup into the lane and shifted into gear. He was only a dozen feet from her. Did he know who she was?

Or was this a random coincidence?

She gave the truck some gas. A little too much, and it zoomed forward.

If she didn't have his attention before, she certainly did now!

She slowed down and watched him in her mirrors as she

approached the street. A woman and little girl exited a minivan in the row behind the one she and the officer had parked in. The child ran to the officer, who swung her up into his arms.

Katie stopped at the street, signaled her turn, then pulled out into traffic. As she drove toward the overpass, she stole a glance back at the officer. The woman gave him a kiss.

He was just there to meet his family!

Her heart was still hammering. She sucked in a long breath and thanked God.

That officer might have noticed her or Zach if he hadn't been focused on seeing his wife and kid.

Driving under the overpass, Katie couldn't see Zach, but knew he wasn't too far ahead. She'd push the speed limit to catch up with him as soon as she could. And he'd probably be driving slow, waiting for her. Hopefully he'd stay on the highway and not pull off to wait.

After the overpass, the highway crossed back into a neighborhood. A marked patrol car sat at an intersection two blocks up.

Had Zach driven past it, staying on the route for Highway 95?

Or had he detoured through the neighborhood, planning to double back to the highway a few blocks farther on? Would the officer notice if he did that?

Katie watched her speedometer, keeping just under the posted limit. The last thing she needed was to be pulled over for speeding, of all things!

She continued up the road, scanning the side streets for any sign of the motorhome. But she didn't see it anywhere.

Where on earth could that man be?

Moments later, she approached the patrol car. The officer's head turned with each vehicle that drove past. He was checking out every person who went by him!

She swallowed. He must be looking for Zach.

And for her.

Lowering the brim of her hat over her sunglasses, she prayed hard.

Oh, Lord Jesus! When you were on earth, you made the blind see. Now, please make seeing eyes blind!

As the FBI agents walked out the driveway, Evan and his parents retreated into their cabin.

"What was all that about?" Mom wondered, leading the way into the living room.

"No idea," Dad said. "But it didn't look good."

"Too bad we can't call and give him a heads up," Evan said.

Mom collapsed onto the sofa. "I keep thinking this day can't get any weirder or worse, and then it does!"

Evan sat in the chair across from her, while Dad strode to the window and peered out toward the driveway.

"Are they coming back?" Mom asked.

"I don't see anybody," he answered. "No agents. No media."

"I hope the ambassador and Elizabeth are alright," Evan said. "You'd have thought Secret Service might have come to take them somewhere safe. That whole FBI thing was... weird."

He didn't have a better word for it.

Had Ambassador Wilford done something suspicious? Did the government think he was somehow involved in the attacks in California or New York?

They actually might. They thought Zach was involved, which was mind blowingly crazy.

If they could suspect Zach, they could suspect anyone. Even the ambassador to Israel.

Or what if they suspected Elizabeth?

Evan couldn't think of any reason why they would – but he didn't really know her. She seemed too young and innocent to be on anyone's radar, though.

What if the FBI took her dad, and left her behind?

Was she scared? Threatened?

He fought back the urge to run right out the front door and sprint to her house. She barely knew him. Besides, the FBI was probably there at the moment and wouldn't look kindly on his barging in. Perhaps he could go check on her later, though.

"I wish there was something we could do." Dad's words broke into his thoughts.

"Me, too!" Mom agreed. "I feel useless. Almost helpless."

Evan sighed. "Well, at least we got some groceries, gas and cash, so we can hunker down for a few days and see what happens."

"Waiting makes it worse," Dad said. "Maybe we should get out of here."

"What? And go where?" Mom asked.

"I don't know." He shrugged and looked back out the window. "Canada?"

Alana had waited long enough. She crossed the room to where the FBI director stood in a huddle with the director of Homeland Security and the CIA chief. They shuffled to create an opening for her.

"We were just discussing the solar storm impact," the CIA boss said.

"Specifically, on our surveillance satellites," Director Chalmers added. "We had to power some of them down before the storm hit."

She met his cold eyes. "And how is that affecting us?"

"Over the western hemisphere, our eyes in the sky are blind."

"So if we're attacked right now, we won't see it coming?" A pain stabbed her stomach.

"We have a lot of other surveillance that would likely pick up on something like that," the CIA director said.

"But we're handicapped," Director Chalmers said. "Like in Nevada, for instance."

The weight of his comment fell on her like a ton of bricks. They couldn't see Zachary Nelson – or his vehicle, now that he'd tripped the license plate reader on the outskirts of Winnemucca.

"Um..." She narrowed her eyes. How much did the CIA and Homeland directors know about the FBI's current operation there? How much should she say in front of them?

She focused on Director Chalmers. "When you have a minute, I need to speak to you. Alone."

"Of course."

Her heart thudded as she turned and walked back to her chair. He better follow her, pronto!

Obviously he hadn't nabbed – or killed – Zachary James Nelson yet. If he had, he would have made it clear.

And now they couldn't even see where he was? How long would that last? How far could he get before the satellites were back online?

Would they be able to find him then?

Or would he be long gone?

Surely that couldn't happen. They were *this close* to catching him in Winnemucca. All the local police should be on alert, along with the county deputies and state troopers, not to mention the FBI had flown in agents. That town was crawling with cops!

He wouldn't be able to evade them.

Alana sank into her chair. How could things go so wrong? When they were so close?

She heaved a sigh and glanced back toward the FBI director. He appeared to be excusing himself from the Homeland / CIA huddle.

Taking a sip of her now-cold coffee, she watched him make his way toward her. He almost sauntered, as if he had not a care in the world.

Well, he'd better start caring! Directors were all replaceable.

"What's the status on our guy?" She asked the moment he was within earshot of her subdued voice.

"Like I told you, he's in Winnemucca. And we can't see where exactly, due to the status of the satellites."

"What you told me was that you'd have him by now," she snapped.

"Look, Winnemucca's not a big town. We've got law enforcement on practically every corner."

"Then you should have eyes on him, shouldn't you?" She stared at him.

He didn't blink. "Mr. Nelson isn't going anywhere. Stop stressing."

That was exactly the wrong thing to say to a strong woman. Alana rose from her chair and leaned toward him.

"I will stop stressing when you stop B.S.-ing me," she hissed.

He raised his hands in faux defense. "I'm not pulling the wool over your eyes. I'm giving it to you straight. I have been, all day."

"All day, you've been telling me you'd have him within the hour. Or within ten minutes." She planted her hands on her hips. "What's it now, five minutes?"

He glanced over his shoulder, as if to see if anyone was listening to their verbal duel.

"Seriously. Settle down," he whispered. "There's no need to make a scene."

"I'm not making a scene!" She said it too loud, and several faces turned her way.

Well, she wasn't before, but she was now. And so what if she was?

"Look, just take care of this. And let me know the second it's done!"

She glared at him for a full three seconds before turning away.

But she was sequestered in the PEOC. Where was she going, exactly?

She beelined for the president, who was seated at the opposite side of the room. Basilia would be happy to have her assistance.

And that snooty FBI guy should be uncomfortable that he was causing her more problems.

As Alana settled into the empty chair next to the president, she cast a quick glance back toward Director Chalmers. He had his back to her, and he was standing at the sandwich table, loading a plate with tiny sandwiches and pickles.

Like he didn't have a care in the world.

CHAPTER TWENTY

Each heartbeat throbbed in Katie's ears as she approached the police officer's parked vehicle, feeling his eyes on her.

Seeing eyes, blind! Seeing eyes, blind, her mind repeated as she felt heat in her face.

Surely the officer would recognize her. Even with the hat and sunglasses. They were hardly a disguise.

He must have her license plate number, too. And be carefully scrutinizing every California plate on his street.

Any moment now, the sound of his siren would scream into her ears, telling the world he'd found her. Found them.

Just as she reached his location, the car ahead of her braked, and Katie had to slow down to avoid a collision. Prolonging her time in front of the officer.

She forced herself not to glance his way – which probably made her even more suspicious, but at least he didn't get the benefit seeing her face straight on. He only saw her profile. And her license plate!

If she got away from here, she and Zach would have to get rid of their plates.

And do what? Drive around plate-less? Steal plates from someone's rig?

Another moment passed, and then she was past the officer.

No siren met her ears. Only the thumping beat of her own heart.

She stole a glance in her mirrors. No flashing lights, either?

He'd let her go by, just like that?

Why?

Because she'd lead him to Zach, that's why! That had to be it. The officer saw that she was alone in the vehicle, and they were really looking for Zach.

They'd track her or follow her until she led them to him.

Katie grimaced. She and Zach would have to split up!

But they already had, sort of. She didn't know where he was. He'd been ahead of her through the underpass, and since then, she hadn't seen him.

There were only two places he could be – either he'd driven right past that police officer and not been apprehended, or he'd taken a side street through the little neighborhood and would have to find a place to re-join Highway 95.

She checked her mirrors again. The officer's vehicle hadn't moved.

Did he radio her in? Was he staying in place to avoid raising her suspicions? Had he called for an unmarked car to follow her out of town?

Or, by some miracle, had he actually not recognized her?

She had prayed for a miracle, after all.

But she couldn't be sure whether she'd gotten one, or whether she'd just been made.

And where was Zach?

She was approaching the end of the neighborhood, and he was nowhere in sight. Soon, she'd be out in the desert. And she didn't dare break radio silence.

The cops were listening.

In fact, maybe they'd heard her and Zach on the walkie talkie in town. They'd used their radio "handles" instead of names, but their conversation was obvious to anybody who might have been listening in.

Katie rolled past the last intersection. Ahead, the speed limit rose to highway speeds.

She glanced in her mirror. The officer hadn't budged.

And her family was still nowhere to be seen.

At Dad's suggestion of going to Canada, Evan found himself astonished into speechlessness. Mom had the opposite reaction.

"Canada?!" She yelped. "What, are you crazy?"

Dad turned slowly from the window and looked at her. "No. Crazy is one thing I'm not!"

Maybe not, but Evan was still shocked at the idea.

"What would we do there?" Mom asked, then pointed toward the kitchen. "I just bought all those groceries!"

Dad came over and sat in the chair beside Evan's.

"Were you listening to anything Ambassador Wilford said?" He focused on Mom. "Things could get seriously bad in the United States."

"You think Canada will just let us in? When our son is a suspected terrorist?" She twisted her hands in her lap.

"There's no reason to think they'll connect us to him. Nelson is a common last name, and we're clear across the country." Dad took a deep breath. "Besides, Evan made us bring our passports when we left home yesterday."

It was true. When Zach called, things sounded so weird, Evan had told his parents to bring their travel documents. Just in case. He'd never dreamed it would come to this, though.

"Look, if the ambassador is wrong, we can come back in a couple days," Dad continued. "Meanwhile, we'll be away from the paparazzi, and we won't have the FBI breathing down our necks. Intentionally or by accident."

Maybe it was a good idea. Or not a really bad one, anyway.

"I don't know...." Mom looked to Evan for – what was she looking for? Support? Input? Advice?

He glanced at Dad, who looked pretty determined.

"What could it hurt?" He wondered aloud. "I mean, like Dad said, if nothing comes of it, we can come back."

"And if the ambassador is right?" Mom asked. "You think Canada will let us stay there? No. They'll toss us out."

"We'll cross that bridge when we come to it," Dad said. "I think we should pack up. We can be in Toronto in about eight hours."

"Now? You want to leave right now?" Mom stared at him. "It's almost dinner time. We'll be driving in the middle of the night!"

Evan glanced at the clock over the fireplace. It was a quarter to five. Almost 2 p.m. where his brother was. Wherever he was. Had he been caught? With Katie and Timothy?

Suddenly, he felt a strong urge to leave.

"Dad's right," he said, rising from the chair. "I think we should get out of here. If Canada lets us in, great! If not, we can come back."

"No, we can't!" Mom objected. "Did you forget the gas lines? You probably won't be able to get any gas to come home. Even if you have enough cash to buy it."

She had a good point. There was a very real possibility that they'd get stranded somewhere. Likely in or near a city, like Pittsburg or Erie or Buffalo.

It might make a lot more sense to sit it out here, in this tiny burg. Maybe, even if Ambassador Wilford was correct, this little community could ride out the danger in relative peace and obscurity.

They were already here. They were safe. They had a little cash, a little food, a little fuel.

They'd give up all that security to travel through dangerous cities at night to attempt to reach another possibly safe location eight hours away in a foreign country. If that all worked out okay, it might possibly be better in the long term. But even that was unknown. As Mom pointed out, Canada might expel them.

Evan bit his lip. Which was the better option?

It was a tough choice. And the wrong decision might get them killed.

As Alana settled into the chair beside the president, the director of Homeland Security was giving an update from the chair opposite her.

"So, while we were missing our eyes in the sky because of the solar storm, it now seems apparent that the nuclear device was delivered by helicopter," he said.

Basilia's fingers curled into fists. "Are you kidding me? A freaking helicopter?!"

He nodded. "At about nine thousand feet. A suicide mission, obviously."

"How?" Basilia's tone deepened. "I mean, how was it in that airspace? How did the bomb get on U.S. soil? Weren't there security checks? Somebody dropped the ball on this, and I want to know who it was!"

"We are looking into all that, of course," the director assured her. "Here's what we think happened – the nuke arrived here by cargo ship, probably from the middle east by way of Europe. The helicopter either came over on that ship, or it was flown onto the ship from one of our East Coast cities."

Making brief eye contact with Alana, he added, "The bomb was loaded onto the bird, which was flown straight over the financial district and detonated. The ship's cargo was never inspected, because it never entered our ports."

"Wait a minute." Alana pressed her fingers to her cheeks. "Are you trying to tell me aircraft can enter the U.S. without any security whatsoever?"

"There are plenty of rules for entering U.S. airspace, of course," he said. "And lots of security for international flights arriving here. But all that was circumvented. It's not too difficult with a helicopter."

"Should we halt all non-government air traffic right now?" Basilia asked. "I mean, what's to prevent a similar attack here in D.C. in ten minutes?"

"That's what I wanted to discuss with you," the director said.

"What's there to discuss? Shut it down!" Basilia's voice rose in pitch and volume. "Now!"

He looked like he wanted to say something more, but then changed his mind. He stood up.

"I'll get started right away."

As he walked away, the president turned to Alana.

"Can you believe that? A helicopter!" Basilia covered her face with her hands.

"Crazy," Alana muttered. What else could she say?

"On my watch." Basilia turned her sharp eyes on her vice president. "I'm going to be blamed for this."

"No, you won't." She protested. "Did you torch California? Did you burst a bomb over New York? No! It's those evil jihadis... I mean, terrorists."

She flinched. Hadn't meant to mention Muslims. Especially since they were painting a target on the back of a Christian for the California attack.

"I will be blamed, though." Basilia's wide eyes filled with tears. "They'll say my administration failed to protect the country."

"Did they do that to President Bush?" Alana asked. "Nope."

"I don't remember. We were pretty young then," the president said. "Anyway, the media is meaner now. Knives will be sharpened, and it's my back they'll be plunged into!"

"The media love you." Alana rubbed Basilia's shoulder. "You're a media darling!"

Basilia blinked, and two tears fell. She wiped them off her cheeks.

"We'll see."

Alana sighed. Basilia was taking this personally, and none of it was her fault. But she wasn't sure what to say to make her feel better. Wine would help, perhaps, but alcohol was out of the question at the moment. When this was all over, though, Alana would send her a bottle of her favorite Merlot.

For now, she tried just changing the topic.

"So what's happening with Dominic and your kids? Have you had a chance to talk to them?"

The president shook her head.

"After the nuke, Secret Service decided not to bring them back to the White House. They're fine." She turned sad eyes on Alana. "I'm glad they're safe, and not here. And I'm glad you are."

Basilia reached for her hand and gave it a squeeze.

CHAPTER TWENTY-ONE

Katie pressed the accelerator reluctantly, and only because two cars were coming up fast behind her. As the pickup began gaining speed, she checked the rearview mirror again.

And saw the motorhome!

Her husband was approaching the highway from the last street in the neighborhood as a semi-truck lumbered past the police car. If Zach timed it right, he might be able to enter the highway in front of the big truck and not be noticed by the officer.

Particularly if the policeman was looking the other direction at that moment.

Katie let off the gas pedal. One of the cars passed her.

As the truck approached him, Zach pulled onto the highway ahead of it.

The next car passed Katie, blasting her with its horn.

She accelerated into a curve, and lost sight of town in her mirrors.

Had Zach gone unnoticed?

In a few seconds, she'd have the answer. Either he'd appear on the highway behind her, or he'd been pulled over.

Please Lord, please Lord, oh, please, Lord!

The Minnie Winnie came around the curve, with the big truck on its tail.

Katie didn't know whether to shout for joy or burst into tears.

She ended up doing both.

As the desert stretched out before her, she wiped her eyes.

That had been a close call. Way, way too close.

Somehow, they had to find a place to hide. But where? And once they got there, how were they going to clear Zach's name?

On the one hand, it seemed like the only way to clear him would be if he turned himself in and answered all their questions. But what if they had no intention of letting him off the hook? What if they were determined to make him a scapegoat?

He'd made a lot of enemies with his blog, that was for sure. He adhered strictly to God's Word, and called out the state and federal government when they didn't. Which was constantly.

The authorities in California hated his guts. They'd be happy to see him burn for this, even though it was most likely one of their own supporters who'd actually torched the state.

What if Zach could never clear his name?

Could they live obscurely in hiding forever?

Where? How?

It probably wasn't even possible.

But she was getting ahead of herself.

To live in hiding, one had to actually hide. She and Zach were still running. That made them extra vulnerable.

They needed to find a place to hunker down. And get there ASAP.

Evan stared blankly at his shoes. How do you make a decision like that? Where the wrong one could cost your life? Or the lives of your family?

He knew how his brother would decide. Zach would pray.

But Evan wasn't into that. Maybe he should be. Maybe he'd learn later.

This Canada decision had to be made now. Today.

In his mind, it was almost a tossup. But he'd rather err on the side of action.

"I think we should go to Canada." He looked his mother in the eye. "I want to go check on the ambassador first, though."

That was a half-truth. He did want to see if Ambassador Wilford was alright, but mostly he wanted to check on his daughter. Elizabeth.

"Do what you want," Dad said. "I'm going to start packing."

"What about our groceries?" Mom asked. "I just bought all that food!"

"Grill some meat, and we'll eat it before we go," Dad said. "I'll bring in the camp cooler from the shed, and you can pack some of the food in that. Maybe not eggs or fresh produce. Canada has all kinds of regulations about what food they'll let you bring in."

"What about canned goods?" Mom asked. "And bread? Crackers?"

"That's probably all fine." He rolled up his sleeves and started for the door. "I'll be back with that cooler."

This was really happening. This entire weekend had been a whirlwind, and it looked like they were buckling in for another ride. Evan froze momentarily while he tried to figure out what to do first.

Probably pack his stuff. He hadn't brought much for the weekend, so it'd only take a minute to pack it.

He bounded up to the loft, gathered his things, and tossed them into his duffel. Then he took a moment to straighten the bed, since he hadn't done that earlier.

Carrying his bag downstairs, he tried to think of anything else he should grab from the cabin.

What if they ended up being in Canada for several weeks? Months? Forever?

What if they had to camp out for a while?

What if they got stranded somewhere enroute to the border, and couldn't make it home again?

Then he'd wish he had a camper on his pickup, along with water filters, guns and ammo. But he didn't have any of that.

Instead, he grabbed the box of matches off the fireplace mantel, some throw blankets and pillows, and a photo album of the family's summers at the cabin. He took all that out to the truck.

When he returned, Mom was taking a plate of meat out to the grill, and Evan squeezed past her into the kitchen. He pulled a couple of sharp knives from the block, wrapped them in a kitchen towel, and put them in a shopping bag. They weren't weapons, exactly, but they could be used for self-defense. Not great, but better than nothing.

He packed up most of the non-perishables Mom had bought earlier, and loaded them in the truck. With the cooler in the back seat and their luggage, the cab would be pretty full. He put his passport in the center console so it would be handy when they arrived at the border.

Had he waited long enough that the FBI would be gone from Ambassador Wilford's place? Probably. Hopefully.

He didn't want to show up while they were still there. Then again, he didn't want to wait too long, either. What if the ambassador and his daughter were being taken away? Or what if they decided to leave on their own after being questioned by the feds?

It was time to go find out. He climbed into the pickup, started the engine, and headed down the road.

Alana took the president's hand in both of hers. "We'll get through this."

Basilia nodded, her eyes wide and wet, as the FBI director approached, carrying his sandwich plate. The man had impeccable timing. In a bad way.

"Quick update," he announced, glancing from Alana to the president. "Our fugitive hasn't tripped the license plate reader leaving Winnemuca yet, and we put drones in the air a few minutes ago."

"I guess that's better than nothing." Basilia's tone was subdued.

"It's great," Director Chalmers enthused. "We've got a lot of boots on the ground, and now we've got eyes in the sky again."

"Fine," Basilia said.

"We're monitoring all the exits, side streets and interstate," he said.

"What if he parks under some trees?" Alana asked.

"Then our agents or local police will catch him. Like I said before, it's a small town." He took a bite of his turkey-Swiss sandwich. "Mmm, these are good!"

He turned and wandered off to talk to the director of Homeland Security.

Alana arched an eyebrow. She'd been trying to boost the president's spirits, but her own confidence was flagging.

Once they took this guy down, she'd feel better, though.

She hated that it was dragging on so long. It gave her conscience time to point its accusing finger at her. Despite her years of suppressing and sloughing off the religion she'd been raised in, some of that forced guilt still pursued her from time to time.

Like today.

Why should she feel guilty?

It had been a tough decision, but it was best for the country. And anyway, it was Basilia's choice in the end, not hers.

If anyone had any guilt to bear – but no one did! They were doing their best here, given the crazy, chaotic circumstances.

Besides, it wasn't like Zachary Nelson was the only innocent person dying today. Millions of his fellow Californians were suffering a far more terrifying, torturous death than he'd face. They were burning to death!

Hour after hour, more people faced the terror of the heat, smoke and unquenchable flames.

And in New York... oh, in New York! She covered her mouth with her hand.

"Are you alright?" The president's question pulled her back from the agony in her mind.

"Those poor people," Alana answered, glancing toward the muted television screen where news images of the ascending mushroom cloud replayed over and over.

"Yeah." Basilia blew out a deep breath. "We would have been there, you know."

"I know!" She turned to study the president's face. "Do you think...?"

"We were targeted?" Basilia shook her head. "Maybe. Probably not. It's so hard to say."

She stared at the images as she continued. "I mean, yes, it was public knowledge that I'd be there this weekend. But I think everybody probably knew that I'd been evacuated last night. You weren't supposed to be there at all."

The president smoothed her dark hair and sighed. "So they weren't after you. And maybe they intended to take me out, and decided to proceed even though I was already relocated. Imagine if I'd still been there, though."

"I can't even think about that!" Alana protested. "Besides, I *was* there with you. So if we hadn't been pulled out last night, we'd both be dead today."

It was a sobering thought. In a weekend filled with sobering thoughts.

What if she'd been killed in that blast?

Her religious upbringing taught that she had a soul that'd be condemned to hell. That was all false, of course. She'd thrown off those beliefs long ago. Her freshman year of college, to be exact.

That had been her year of freedom. Of abandoning restraints and rules and religious objections.

Looking back, it had been the best year of her life. So far.

Still, while she refused to believe in God or religion anymore, she couldn't prove, even to herself, that God did not exist.

And she'd never been able to totally abolish Pascal's Wager from her mind. It made a strong rational argument for believing in God, regardless of whether or not his existence could be proven.

That bothered her. A lot. She was a rational person, after all. What if her disbelief was irrational? If she was wrong, and God was real, she was setting herself up for eternal disaster.

She stood up and reached for the President's empty coffee cup. "How about a refill?"

CHAPTER TWENTY-TWO

Katie scanned the highway ahead, checking each oncoming vehicle to see if it looked like law enforcement. Tension tightened her shoulders as she drove the long, straight stretch of asphalt in the desert. The pickup's air conditioner blew frigid air on her arms, but her face still felt hot.

Static crackled her walkie talkie.

"Let's take the next left, Mermaid," Zach said. She could barely make out his words, because the transmission kept cutting out.

A sign indicated an upcoming intersection with State Route 140.

"Roger that," Katie answered. Hopefully he'd heard her.

Zach had the maps, so she didn't know where this highway would take them. Maybe she should ask. Then again, it was probably best to stay off the airwaves as much as possible. And the radios didn't seem to be working very well, either.

Besides, she didn't really care where the new highway went. At this point, she just wanted to put miles between her family and any populated area. Population meant police. And police meant trouble.

She flicked on her blinker and touched her brakes, then turned onto the two-lane state route. She glanced in her rearview mirror. After waiting for an oncoming Jeep, Zach followed her.

The highway ahead would take them west. Back toward California.

She swallowed. That was one place she didn't want to be! The fires, the closed highways... they could easily get trapped.

The highway made a slight bend to the right, moving a little toward the north.

Once around that bend, she saw another curve to the right in the distance. That could make their travel direction northwest, possibly taking them into southeast Oregon.

She could live with that.

If they could get away from this dry, barren desert and eventually find some forest, they might be able to hide. The feds were probably searching for them with satellites or drones. Being under a canopy of trees would help shield her family from the eyes in the skies.

But they were a long way from anything like that. Mile upon mile of bleak desert stretched out ahead of her.

Nevertheless, God had protected them so far. They were still running, still free.

Maybe he had a plan for them, a place to hide them. Like Psalm 91 said.

She searched her memory for the words. A few years ago, she'd struggled to memorize the chapter, but now only bits and pieces came back to her.

There was something about abiding in the shelter of God's wings. It reminded her of a mother hen gathering her chicks under the safety of her feathers.

After a moment, she remembered the first two verses.

"He who dwells in the secret place of the Most High shall abide under the shadow of the Almighty," she whispered. "I will say of the Lord, 'He is my refuge and my fortress; my God, in Him I will trust.'"

She inhaled and slowly expelled the breath, feeling her muscles relax at the same time.

Yes, she would trust him. But how exactly did one go about dwelling in the secret place of the Most High?

It was a question she mulled over as one dry mile followed another. The desert seemed endless. After being in it for a while, it was hard to imagine anything else existed besides dry rocks, sand and dust. It was all she could see.

And yet, she knew there was more to this earth than desert. Just yesterday, she'd been at the ocean. It seemed so long ago, so distant and carefree compared to her current situation.

Life was like that sometimes. When she was in a crisis, it was hard to believe it would come to an end and everyday normality would return. But it always did.

During troubled times, her mom had a favorite saying: "This, too, shall pass."

She'd said it often when teenaged Katie had a bad day and couldn't imagine life would ever straighten out again. But Mom was right. Those teenaged dramas did come to an end.

Was it possible that this weekend's crisis would resolve, as well?

That was very difficult to imagine. Very difficult, indeed!

Evan pulled into the ambassador's driveway. The only vehicles he saw were Elizabeth's Audi and her dad's SUV. The FBI agents must have left. Or they'd parked farther away from the house.

He opened his door and climbed out, then slammed the door. He didn't want to surprise them.

Watching the home's windows, he saw no movement as he strode to the front door.

Perhaps the FBI had taken them away.

He knocked on the door. "Hello? Ambassador Wilford?"

Footsteps approached.

Elizabeth's face appeared in the door's window. She didn't smile. A deadbolt scraped as she turned the lock, then opened the door.

"Is everything okay?" He asked. "The FBI came to our place –"

"They took Dad!" Tears edged her green eyes.

"Why?"

"I'm not sure. They didn't actually arrest him... but they were rude and insistent."

Evan rubbed the stubble on his jaw. "They didn't indicate what it was about?"

"They said the president wanted to see him." She frowned. "I guess they couldn't reach him on the phone."

"Which he left at our place," Evan said.

"Phones aren't working anyway. Between the panic and the solar storm, the connections are either busy or malfunctioning." She took a step back, pulling the door fully open. "Would you like to come in?"

"I'd love to, but I can't stay. We're getting ready to go to Canada."

"Really?" Her big eyes widened. "Now?"

He nodded. If only he could invite her to come along, and not sound weird asking.

"As soon as we have a bite to eat and get packed," he said. "Dad's grilling some steak. You're welcome to join us."

"For dinner," she clarified.

"And to Canada, if you want." He said it before he'd figured out how he'd say it. Oh, well. It was out there now.

Her eyebrows shot up, wrinkling her forehead. This was quickly replaced by a small, bemused smile.

"My dad just got picked up by the FBI, and you're asking if I want to take an international trip? Tonight?"

"I didn't expect you to take me up on it," he said. "I was just being nice."

That wasn't even a half truth. He totally wished she would join them.

"Anyway, if your dad is right, we don't think we should stay in the U.S. to wait for things to get worse," he added. "We're going to try to get out now."

"I see." A thoughtful look crossed her face. "That may not be a bad idea. I hope it all works out."

Meaning, she wasn't coming along. Understandably.

"Thanks." He shifted his weight. "Anyway, I wanted to check on you guys before we left. And you *are* welcome to come over for dinner."

She leaned against the doorframe. "I appreciate the offer. But I'm a vegetarian, and you're grilling beef."

"Oh. Okay."

Why couldn't he think of a single intelligent thing to say? He swallowed and tried to make his mouth work.

"So, uh, I guess I'll be going, then." He tried to smile, but he was sure it looked fake.

"Thanks for stopping by." She lifted her chin. "Good luck. With everything."

"Thanks. You, too." He turned and stepped off her porch before he could stick his foot in his mouth again.

Why did he have such a struggle with words when she was around?

Alana sighed as she filled the president's coffee cup and her own. It felt like this crisis would never end.

What if it didn't?

What if, instead of the crisis ending, America itself came to an end?

Of course that was impossible. Ridiculous. Countries weather crises, they don't just fold up and flop over. People still live there, and governments continue to govern.

But not always, right? Throughout history, lots of countries and civilizations have perished. They were gone from the face of the earth, only known now through archeology and artifacts.

What had happened to them? Famine. Disease. Conquest.

That was not the case here. At least not the first two.

But conquest?

Were these attacks on America part of an enemy's broader plan to destroy the government and take over the country?

She spilled some coffee, and reached for the stack of napkins.

"Are you okay?" Basilia appeared at her elbow and reached for her cup.

Alana leaned toward the president and whispered. "What if we're not looking at this right?"

"How so?" The president took a sip of coffee.

"What if this isn't just a terrorist attack? What if we're about to be invaded?"

Basilia's eyebrows arched. "By whom? I don't see any armies lined up at our borders."

"Well, no," Alana agreed. "But imagine if this was a joint Iranian/Russian plan? Iran sponsors the California attack and lobs the nuke at New York, while Russia lies off in the weeds and waits for a moment when we're weak."

Basilia's gaze fastened on her. "Then what? How are they going to get their army here without us knowing?"

"But that's what I'm saying," she protested. "We might know, but be too weak to repel invaders."

"That'll be the day!" The president scoffed. "It'll never happen. We can always launch our nukes, and they know it."

Alana wasn't so sure, but it was time to drop it. Basilia wasn't ready to think strategically yet; she was still caught up in the shock of the crisis. Give her a day or two, though, and she'd be putting her brilliant brain power on all the possibilities.

"Good news!" The FBI director's voice boomed right behind her. Alana turned abruptly, sloshing her coffee. It barely stayed in the mug.

"That's what I like to hear." Basilia focused on him. "Tell me."

"We've picked up Ambassador Wilford," Director Chalmers said.

"Good!" Basilia almost smiled. "How soon will he be here?"

"Within the hour. He's on a plane now."

"Let me know the moment he arrives," the president said. "I have a lot of questions for that man."

Alana sipped her coffee. Soon, the ambassador would have his opportunity to talk to the president. Whether he wanted to or not, at this point. Last night, he'd been so insistent.

Would he feel the same way today, now that New York had been hit?

He was probably wishing he was in Jerusalem right now, not on his way to the bunker under the White House.

CHAPTER TWENTY-THREE

The desert seemed to stretch on forever. Katie squirmed in her seat, then straightened her back, then rolled her shoulders.

She'd emptied her water bottle half an hour ago. Now, her stomach rumbled. A snack would be nice.

Could they afford to pull off for a quick break? She was eager to find a good hideout, but she also needed to use the bathroom in the motorhome. It would just take a minute.

She reached for the walkie talkie and keyed the mic.

"Runner? You have your ears on?"

"Roger that, Mermaid. Go ahead." Heavy static crackled the transmission as Zach spoke.

"I need to stop for a minute."

A pause. More static.

" –right. Find a place, and I'll follow you."

"You're breaking up," she said.

"Okay. Let's stop."

The narrow highway's shoulder widened ahead, and Katie applied her brakes and signaled to turn off there.

Zach pulled in behind her as she stopped. The eight-foot-wide

RV was mostly out of the travel lane, and traffic on this highway was sparse at best.

Katie grabbed her water bottle, hopped out of the pickup and hurried into the motorhome. Timothy was dozing in his car seat. Zach turned around and looked at her.

Rather than say anything that would wake up their son, she just pointed toward the bathroom. Zach nodded.

"I'll take Duke out," he whispered.

She gave him a thumbs up and headed to the back of the RV.

When she returned, Zach was bringing the dog back in, and Timothy was awake.

"Mommy!" He held his arms out to her.

"Hi, sweetheart." Without releasing him from the booster seat, she gave him a hug and a kiss. "Mommy loves you."

"Let's have cookies!"

That child! Always thinking about food. But cookies did sound pretty good.

"Yeah, let's!" His father agreed.

That man! Katie smiled in spite of herself. She stepped into the tiny kitchen and pulled a box of chocolate chip cookies from the cabinet.

"I was saving these for tomorrow," she said. "How'd you guys even know they were there?"

"We have our ways." Zach winked and held out his hand.

She handed him two cookies. "One of those is for your son."

"Aww..." With great exaggeration, his shoulders drooped. "Okay...."

He took a big bite of one of the cookies, then handed the rest of it to Timothy.

"Zachary James Nelson!" As she spoke the words, she was reminded of the media reports using her husband's full name.

His face darkened. He must be thinking the same thing.

"I'm sorry," she said.

"It's okay. We should get going." He hurried up to the driver's seat and settled in. "How're you doing for gas?"

"I'm fine for now. You?" She filled her water bottle.

"Same." He took a huge bite of his cookie.

She started out the door, and the motorhome rocked as a semi blasted past it. She couldn't wait to get off the road.

Back in the pickup, she pulled into the traffic lane. The highway was almost as deserted as the desert itself. Maybe one car a minute went by in the opposite direction. Almost nobody was going her way.

It felt like a small mercy, and she was thankful for it.

In an otherwise merciless weekend, she was glad for any break they could get.

Evan was polishing off his plate of steak and salad when he heard a vehicle turn in the driveway. He tensed. Now what?

Mom set down her fork. "Who do you suppose –"

"I'll go see." He wiped his mouth with a napkin and stood up.

Approaching the door, he could see a dark blue vehicle through the window. Could it be? His breath stalled momentarily.

He pulled the door open and stepped out onto the porch. It was! Elizabeth!

She parked her Audi beside his pickup. Her door opened. He hurried toward her.

"Is everything okay?" He asked as she got out, the low sun highlighting her long auburn hair.

"Yes." She glanced toward the cabin pensively. "I know this is crazy, but...."

Evan held his breath. What if? Could she possibly...?

"Go ahead," he urged after her sentence stalled out. Maybe she'd changed her mind! Perhaps she would come with them! His heart thumped as his hopes soared.

"Well." She frowned slightly. "I think it may be a good idea to leave the country."

"With me?" He asked. "I mean, with us? To Canada?"

Huge green eyes studied him for a long moment. Then she nodded.

"Yes."

That one word made him almost giddy. He couldn't restrain the grin that was quickly taking over his face. He felt like a geeky teenager. And probably looked like one at the moment, too. He covered his mouth, trying to hide his obvious delight.

"I think that's a good idea." He tried to sound restrained, but his pitch was too high. Lowing it, he added, "We're just about ready to take off. Do you want to ride with us?"

There was hardly room in the pickup, with the three Nelsons and their luggage.

"No, I'll take my own car."

Mom and Dad came out of the cabin.

"Elizabeth is going to Canada with us," he explained.

"You have your passport?" Dad asked.

She nodded. "We travel a lot, so I take it with me whenever we leave town."

"What happened with your dad?" Mom came down the steps. "The FBI?"

"The president wanted to see him. They were escorting him to D.C."

Concern etched Mom's face. "But everything's okay?"

"I suppose. I don't really know." Elizabeth sighed. "Honestly, nothing about this weekend is okay."

She pressed her lips together for a moment, then took a quick breath.

"Anyway. I'm packed and ready. I sent an email and a text to Dad, so hopefully he'll get my message and know where I'm going."

"I'm sure he will," Mom said. "We just ate, but I could make you a plate –"

"No, thanks, I'm fine." Elizabeth waved her off. "I already ate."

Dad approached the front of her car and shielded his eyes from the sun. "I think it's good you're coming. Now we won't have to worry about you."

He shifted his gaze to give Evan a pointed look.

Evan turned toward Mom.

"So... are we about ready to go?"

A disturbance at the door caught Alana's attention. FBI agents escorted Ambassador Wilford into the PEOC, then Secret Service agents flanked him as the FBI guys withdrew, closing the door behind them.

The ambassador was dressed casually, in a short-sleeved white cotton shirt and khaki pants. Alana was sure she'd never seen him without a suit and tie.

Silence fell across the room as his old blue eyes turned toward the president, who stood inches from Alana's shoulder. Something about his gaze rattled her.

Had he known this nuclear attack was coming? Had he participated somehow?

"You decided to see me," he announced, adjusting his bifocals. "Last night, you apparently had no time. And yesterday, you were in a hurry."

Alana bristled. That was no way to speak to the president of the United States. Who did this guy think he was?

Basilia lifted her chin. "You left a strange message with Vice President Mills."

"Because she wouldn't put you on the phone," he said, shifting his gaze to Alana. His look was unsettling, to the point that she had a difficult time maintaining eye contact.

Finally, he turned his gaze back to the president, and Alana was able to regain her composure.

Basilia's back straightened as she glanced toward the Secret Service agents beside him. "We'll speak in the small conference room."

"You're afraid to let your cabinet hear what I'm going to say?" The old man's look was incredulous.

"My team has work to do," the president said. "They don't need to hear every theory from every bureaucrat."

She pointed toward the door of the smaller room, and the agents whisked him into it.

"Alana, you're with me," Basilia said. "And Director Chalmers."

The FBI director held the door open for them. The room contained only a small table and four chairs, and the ambassador was taking a seat at the far end.

With a sharp look and a wave of her finger, Basilia sent the security team out. She took the seat opposite the ambassador, so Alana and Dick Chalmers seated themselves across from each other.

The air conditioner kept the room at a reasonable temperature, but something felt stifling. Maybe Alana was developing some claustrophobia or something. Avoiding the ambassador's eyes, she took a long, deep breath and focused on releasing it slowly.

"Now, then." The president crossed her arms. "Tell me everything you know."

"Very well." The ambassador leaned forward, resting his arms on the table. "As I explained yesterday, the Israelis –"

"No, no, no!" Basilia hissed. "Israel had nothing to do with this! We know that much."

A perplexed look crossed the ambassador's face. "They certainly didn't launch the attacks, if that's what you mean. But I think Israel has everything to do with it."

Alana set her coffee on the table. The old man was talking gibberish again. This was a waste of time, just as she expected.

"Explain," the president demanded.

"As I said yesterday, they are furious about America's betrayal when their enemies attacked in April. And as I mentioned yesterday, they may have laid curses on our country. Or on you."

His eyes never wavered from the president's. A shiver trembled Alana's spine.

"Go on." Basilia's tone was pure ice.

"As I told Vice President Mills –" his gaze shifted to Alana – "This weekend's attacks may be the opening scenes in America's demise. The Jewish prophets –"

"Prophets? Are you kidding me?" The president rose to her feet. "Come on! I need facts here. Real information!"

"I'm giving you all I've got." The ambassador spread his hands. "I warned the vice president about this last night, and then New York was attacked today. You think I'm making this up?"

She stared at him, but said nothing.

"You're the one who brought me here. Do you want to hear what I have to say, or not?"

CHAPTER TWENTY-FOUR

Katie drove through the Sheldon National Wildlife Refuge, but didn't see a single animal in it. Maybe because it was in the afternoon and the animals were smart enough to lay low during the heat of the day. Or maybe they avoided the highway slicing through the middle of their refuge. In any case, it just looked like more hot, dry desert to her.

Then the highway swung north and a sign announced they were entering Oregon.

Finally!

It looked exactly the same, of course, but Oregon held promise that northwest Nevada didn't. Specifically, forests that she and Zach could hide in with Timothy and Duke. Cooler temperatures, maybe, and rain, and the ocean.

Not that she'd be going to the beach, obviously, but Oregon seemed like a refuge compared to Nevada.

At some point, they'd need to stop and get gas. She glanced at her gauge. It hovered just over a third of a tank. The motorhome was a gas guzzler, so it'd need fuel soon, too.

And there was no way on earth she was going to repeat yesterday's experience of running out!

A few minutes later, she drove into a fertile valley. Lots of irrigation had produced green fields. A sign indicated the approach to Greaser Reservoir.

Seriously? Greaser? There had to be a story behind that name!

She didn't see a gas station in the small community, though.

Leaving the valley, the highway began a series of curves as it climbed in elevation. Higher and higher, and suddenly there were trees!

A forest!

Katie scanned for side roads. Maybe there was someplace they could get off the beaten path and hide out.

She spotted a few logging roads, but none that seemed like a good road to take the RV. There were a few other roads that looked like county roads – but she didn't want to draw attention to her family by parking alongside a road where everybody knew everybody. They needed to find a place where they could remain anonymous.

And dye their hair, as soon as she was able to purchase some hair color.

Soon, the winding road began a descent, and eventually it dead-ended onto a north-south highway.

Which way should they go?

She glanced in her mirror, but Zach was still almost a quarter-mile behind her. The sign indicated the town of Lakeside to the south.

Maybe they could get gas there.

She flicked on her blinker for the left-hand turn. As Zach approached, he signaled the same, so he must be fine with it.

She pulled out onto the quiet two-lane highway and drove south through the valley. Homes dotted the sides of the road, and farms produced green, irrigated fields.

In just a couple of minutes, she was pulling into town.

She searched for a gas station.

Driving slowly, she passed an inn, a motor lodge, and a coffee company. Then the highway split, with part of it continuing south, and the other part heading west.

Preferring to head toward the ocean and mountains, rather than back toward Nevada or California, she took the right-hand turn toward the west.

She drove by a dollar store, an antique store, a fast-food joint, a motel, a bakery. Where on earth were the gas stations in this town?

Everybody knows the gas stations are supposed to be located along the highways, right?

Right?

Evan pulled onto the highway, glancing in his mirror to make sure Elizabeth was still behind the pickup. She was. He turned his gaze forward, but couldn't get her out of his thoughts.

Was she nuts? Traveling with a family she barely knew?

On the other hand, she'd known the Nelsons all her life. Just not very well. Especially over the past ten years.

Anyway, she wasn't putting her life in their hands. She was traveling in her own car, so she could strike out on her own at any point. She retained her autonomy, while attaching herself to the safety of a larger group.

That was just plain smart.

She had a good head on her shoulders. Had she always?

He couldn't remember. His main recollections of her were of an annoying little kid. She'd obviously outgrown that stage!

She might have a boyfriend. Probably did, in fact.

Was there any way to find out, without being an idiot? He'd sounded like one enough today already.

The trees that lined the curve ahead had turned yellow, and now they glowed like gold in the setting sun. It was a nice evening. Hard to believe the world was crashing around their ears, when everything looked so normal. Beautiful, even.

Beside him, Mom let out a long sigh. Evan glanced at her. From the backseat, Dad put his hand on her shoulder and gave it squeeze.

"We'll be okay," he promised.

Would they? Evan had his doubts.

If they found enough gas to get to Canada, and were admitted at the border, maybe they'd be okay. But a lot of time and miles stood between now and then. Perhaps a lot of danger, too.

Were they wrong to be traveling at night?

A lot of the people on the roads at night were drunk or dangerous or up to no good. It seemed like a bad time to be driving.

On the other hand, if they waited until morning, it might be impossible. Gasoline might be unavailable, people would be even more desperate, and there might be hordes of them trying to go somewhere safe.

Someplace like Galloway. Which the Nelsons were abandoning, in hopes of something elsewhere that might be better.

Evan frowned. Hopefully, this wasn't one colossal mistake.

Returning to the summer cabin tomorrow or the next day would be challenging, to say the least. And if they did make it back, they might find that squatters had settled in. What would they do in that case?

"Maybe we could listen to some music," Mom said, turning on the radio.

A lot of static crackled through the speakers. She tried another station, and found one that came in better. As the last strains of a song ended, the announcer came on.

"U.S. markets will be closed tomorrow, but Asian and European markets are expecting a bloodbath as they open tonight. Futures are down over fifteen percent in most exchanges," he said. "Meanwhile, the crises on both ends of the country are worsening. In California, the death toll will not be known for months, but it's clearly increasing at an alarming rate as the fires rage across the state. And in New York, survivors are attempting to get help."

His voice cut out as he continued. "— are arriving at clinics and emergency rooms with broken bones, massive lacerations, and third-degree burns, as well as radiation poisoning. Hospitals are overwhelmed, even as they try to evacuate patients from the fallout region."

He drew a quick breath. "In both states, families are trying to locate their loved ones. However, since communication systems are barely functional, this is proving to be an impossible task. Telecommunication infrastructure in both regions have been destroyed, and the rest of the country's networks are hampered by unprecedented high demand and a moderate solar storm."

The broadcast segued into a commercial.

Evan turned the volume down a bit.

"Good heavens!" Mom reached for a tissue. "And not a word about your brother."

"That might be good," Dad said. "I think they'd mention it if they had picked him up."

"You would think so," Evan agreed.

Coming up the onramp, he merged with traffic northbound on I-79. He checked his rearview mirror. Elizabeth was still right behind him. Almost tailgating, actually.

Was she one of *those* drivers?

Hopefully she'd notice if he had to slam on his brakes. It'd be awful if she rear-ended him. Maybe he should suggest that she take the lead.

If *he* were in the following vehicle, he'd be certain not to run into her little sedan.

Alana shrank back in her seat as the president glared at Ambassador Wilford. The room was growing hotter by the second.

"I don't want to hear about ancient prophets, I want to hear whether you were involved in this!" Basilia remained standing, planting her hands on the table and leaning toward the ambassador. "Did you have some kind of prior knowledge?"

"My only prior knowledge, if it could be called that, comes from the ancient manuscripts," he said. "If I and others are interpreting those prophecies correctly, the United States is at this moment poised for destruction."

"In a single day?" Basilia sat down. "Are we going to be hit again? Who is the aggressor?"

"A single day, a single hour..." he gave a slight nod. "I don't know who attacked us, or whether they'll hit us again."

"What good are you, then?" the president huffed. "I need answers!"

"Answers won't help at this point." His eyes never left her face.

"Of course they will!" She paused, then frowned. "What do you mean?"

"All the answers in the world won't change our situation, if we are the nation spoken of by the prophets. We will fall in a cataclysmic, spectacular fashion, and there's nothing that can be done to prevent it."

She stared at him in silence.

"I reject that. We're done here!" She rose, turned swiftly, and exited the room.

Alana watched the door slam shut.

Now what? Should she get up and leave, too?

Probably. But her curiosity was piqued, and she'd never been one to deny her curiosity. The FBI director stood and headed out the door, but Alana turned her gaze to the ambassador.

"Tell me about the prophecies," she said.

He leaned forward, and his eyes seemed to be filled with energy.

"Our time here is short. You must find a Bible, and read Revelation chapter 18. It describes the fall of Mystery Babylon, which you will recognize as America. Then read the parallel prophecies in Jeremiah chapters 50 and 51, which refer to the Daughter of Babylon."

Alana leaned back and crossed her arms. "I have all the time in the world. Explain it to me."

He raised one eyebrow, but reached into his pocket and pulled out a tiny, leather-bound book. Flipping toward the back, he found his page and adjusted his bifocals.

"This is from Revelation 18, regarding Mystery Babylon. Since we're short on time, I'll start with verse seven."

"We're not short on time!" Alana nearly rolled her eyes.

He shrugged and began reading.

"In the measure that she glorified herself and lived luxuriously, in the same measure give her torment and sorrow; for she says in her heart, 'I sit as queen, and am no widow, and will not see sorrow. Therefore her plagues will come in one day – death and mourning and famine. And she will be utterly burned with fire, for strong is the Lord God who judges her."

A shiver spun up Alana's spine as images of California's fires and New York's devastation filled her mind. The ambassador continued reading.

"The kings of the earth who committed fornication and lived luxuriously with her will weep and lament for her, when they see the smoke of her burning, standing at a distance for fear of her torment, saying, 'Alas, alas, that great city Babylon, that mighty city! For in one hour your judgment has come –"

The door flew open and the president pinned Alana with a fierce look.

"Come out here! I need you."

Alana rose from her chair as the ambassador spoke.

"Like I said, we were short on time." He stood up. "Revelation chapters 17 and 18. Jeremiah 50 and 51."

Alana moved toward the door without looking back. A magnetic force was pulling her to the president's side.

CHAPTER TWENTY-FIVE

Katie finally spotted a gas station at the end of town. It wasn't very big, but several vehicles were at the pumps and parked in front of the store. Hopefully the motorhome would be able to fit in at the pumps.

She turned in and tried to forget the hassle she'd had this morning at a similar little convenience store when she'd purchased the road maps. Thank God that nosy woman didn't ever figure out who Katie was!

Zach pulled in at the pump next to her, and rolled down his window as she walked over.

"Glad you saw this place," he said. "We were getting pretty low."

"Me, too." She glanced apprehensively at the building. "I'll have to go inside and prepay. Would you pray they don't recognize me?"

Zach took her hand and offered up a quick power prayer. She felt courage seep into her spirit.

She inhaled deeply. "Okay."

"Go get 'em, Babe!" Zach smiled. "But keep your sunglasses on."

She strode toward the building, shoulders square but stomach tense. The clerk, a young man who barely looked old enough to have graduated from high school, finished with the customer at the counter, then looked at her.

"Gas on pumps 6 and 7, please," she said in as steady a voice as she could manage.

"We're only taking cash." The gangly cashier glanced out the window toward the motorhome. Then took her money and turned on the pumps.

Katie hurried back out and started fueling the rigs.

"I feel like a cad for not pumping the gas," Zach said from his open window.

"Don't you dare get out of that RV!" Katie glanced his way. "The last thing we need is somebody spotting you."

"I still feel like a cad," he said.

"You can make it up to me later." Trying to look natural for anyone who might be watching, she forced a smile.

Finally, the pump for the pickup clicked off. She hung up the nozzle and waited for the motorhome to finish fueling. That thing had a huge, thirsty, expensive gas tank.

Keeping her head low, she glanced around the lot.

So far, so good. Nobody seemed to be paying her and Zach any particular attention. She looked back toward the store.

Glare off the windows prevented her from seeing clearly inside, but what she did see chilled her.

It looked like that kid cashier was on the phone. And like he was looking at her.

Time to go!

She turned off the pump, hung up the nozzle, and spoke quietly to Zach.

"We might have been made. I'm going inside, but be ready to take off the minute I get done!"

"Got it." He turned on the engine as she hurried back into the store.

As she entered, the cashier was speaking quietly, and looking at her. Instantly, he turned away.

Her face warmed and her heart thumped.

And there was a line at the counter! Only three people, but still – if he was talking to the cops, and took his time with all these people, the police could be here before she finished.

What if she just left?

Yeah, nothing suspicious about that! Not knowing how much it would cost to fill both tanks, she'd overpaid by more than forty dollars. Nobody would walk off and leave that kind of money with the clerk.

Her heart sank as she got into line.

Finally, he hung up the phone and started ringing up the first customer. A bag of chips, two bottles of pop, a pack of cigarettes, and when she thought he was finally finished, he added a gas pump purchase!

Katie glanced outside. Zach had rolled up his window, which was probably a good idea.

Her ears strained for police sirens, but she heard nothing. Probably wouldn't hear it here in the store until it was too late, anyway.

The first customer left, and the second one stepped up to the counter.

Katie's face had gone from warm to hot, and now her pulse was hammering in her ears. She wanted nothing more than to run from this place and race away up the road.

How much had that gas cost, anyway? The truck had taken around $75, and she'd stopped the RV pump at around $120 – it wasn't completely full, but it was enough to get far from here.

If they had time.

Evan's plan was to stay on I-79 north through Pittsburg, clear up to Erie, where they could connect with I-90 and follow that interstate along the northeast edge of the lake to Buffalo. Then they'd cross the border at their first opportunity.

It appeared to be the fastest, most direct route. Especially if traffic didn't get too snarled up tonight.

Erie was less than 250 miles from Galloway, so he hoped to make it in less than five hours, even if traffic was problematic.

It'd be good to keep the gas tank topped off every few hours, if possible. So rather than use rest areas for bathroom breaks, he'd pull off at 24-hour gas stations.

At least, that was his plan.

If all went well.

He glanced in his mirror. Elizabeth was still plastered on his bumper.

Great. He touched his brakes to flash his brake lights, and she backed off. Slightly.

Then after a moment, she attached her Audi to his bumper again.

Yeah. He'd definitely suggest she take the lead, if she was going to drive like that.

His thoughts turned to his brother. Had Zach been caught? What would happen to Katie and Timothy?

If he was arrested, Evan would want to be there for him. And for his family. But here he was, driving to Canada, of all places. So hopefully Zach had gotten his message and had ditched his cell phone and the interstates.

Evan sighed. He glanced at his mother. She was swiping at her cell phone. She turned it his direction and took a picture. He didn't smile.

Well, if you couldn't make a call on the darn thing, you could still use it as a camera.

He couldn't call or text his brother... was there another way to communicate? Social media was out, since he was pretty sure accessing it would reveal Zach's location.

What about Zach's political/religious blog? Had it been taken down?

If not, could Evan leave a reply – in code, of course – to one of the recent posts?

Would Zach see it? He might not check his blog for days or weeks, if he was still free, for fear of being traced.

Maybe he should just wait for Zach to contact him when he was safe.

If he didn't get caught.

Evan gritted his teeth. He was pretty sure that if Zach did get arrested, it'd be on the news. So he'd make a point of listening to all the hourly updates.

And hope to not hear the one thing he was dreading.

———

"What were you doing?" Basilia hissed.

Startled, Alana met her gaze. "I wanted to hear what the ambassador had to say."

"He only had nonsense. I'd hoped he had some real intel. No such luck." Her expression softened and she put her hand on Alana's shoulder. "I need you to stay focused. California. New York. And especially Zachary James Nelson."

"I'm on it."

"Good." The president turned and struck up a conversation with the CIA director.

Alana glanced back to the small conference room, where Secret Service agents were escorting the ambassador out the door. Almost like he was a suspect. Or a criminal.

The old man turned and made eye contact with her. He lifted his chin as if to acknowledge her presence and position. Then he shuffled out of the PEOC, surrounded by agents.

As the doors swung shut, she sensed a power shift in the room. The energy had changed. What was up with that?

The ambassador held an important position, but not a powerful one. It didn't make sense, then, that his presence could move the energy in the PEOC.

But she didn't have time to think about esoteric matters like that. She had real issues to deal with, as the president had pointed out.

California. New York. Zachary Nelson.

Her mood darkened.

For a moment, she wished she'd never accepted the position of vice president. She should have stayed in her cushy job in Congress. Lots of wealth, lots of power, none of the blame for things gone wrong.

And no need to find and then hunt down innocent scapegoats.

Ugh! She shoved the thoughts aside.

The president had made a choice.

Alana was just doing her job. And the sooner she got it done, the sooner she could stop thinking about it. She turned her focus to the FBI director, who stood across the room with his back to her.

That man had better have some good news by now!

As if he had eyes in the back of his head and saw her coming, he made a beeline for the door leading to the restrooms. A moment later, Basilia caught Alana's eye and beckoned her over. She was talking with the secretaries of Health and Human Services, and Homeland Security.

Alana hurried to the president's side.

"We're getting an update on the health issues facing New York," Basilia explained.

"So, as I was saying, we're trying to evacuate the hospitals outside the blast zone. To move people away from the fallout region," the HHS secretary said. "However, they are being flooded by waves of patients coming out of the city. Most of whom are contaminated. They have radioactive fallout on their clothes, in their hair, everywhere."

The Homeland Security director jumped in. "We need to quarantine and decontaminate everybody, but it's too chaotic. There are literally thousands of contaminated people running around all over the place. They're trying to escape the fallout, but they're bringing it with them. To hospitals, gas stations, public transportation –"

"It's a nightmare!" The HHS secretary put his palms to his temples. "We've got to do something. As the ash and dust falls off them, they're contaminating every place they go!"

"Exactly. They're exposing people who weren't anywhere near the fallout areas," the Homeland director said. "As they move away from the epicenter, they're contaminating busses, trains, their own vehicles... soon it will be hotels, restaurants and hospitals all over the East Coast!"

Basilia cussed. "So, what do you want? Martial law?"

"Yes!" Both men said in unison.

"It's the only way to reign this in, protect the citizens and manage the crisis," the HHS director said. "And we need it immediately!"

"Fine," the president agreed. "Talk to Defense and get it rolling."

CHAPTER TWENTY-SIX

Katie tried not to stare out the gas station window, watching for the inevitable police vehicles. It was silly to listen for sirens. No doubt they'd approach silently, to avoid alerting their prey.

Hopefully Zach was praying up a storm out there.

After an eternity, the second customer left, and the one in front of Katie stepped up to the counter. With a basket full of convenience store junk food, plus a loaf of bread and a carton of milk.

The skinny young cashier rang up each article slowly and finally read off the total.

"Eighteen dollars and sixty-seven cents." He shifted his eyes toward the gas pumps. Where Zach was.

The customer, a middle-aged woman with greying hair, pulled a card from her wallet.

"Cash only," the clerk said in a bored voice.

The woman began rummaging through her purse, pulling out a five dollar bill, three ones, and several quarters. She set each one on the counter, one at a time.

Goodness!

She'd never get out of here. The forces of darkness had

converged to stall every transaction, to delay every customer, to prevent Katie and Zach from getting away before the cops came.

If they were actually coming.

Katie tried to quell the panic in her heart. She didn't know whom the clerk had been talking to on the phone.

It might be his manager, or his grandmother, for all she knew.

"That's all I've got," the lady said. "Eight dollars and seventy-five cents."

The cashier looked at the woman as if he had no idea what to do.

"I guess I don't need the candy," the lady said.

"Here." Katie pulled a ten dollar bill from her wallet. She held it out to the cashier.

"What?" The woman turned around and looked at her. "You don't have to do that."

"It's okay." She nodded to the cashier. "Go ahead."

He rang the sale through the register and handed Katie a few coins.

"Thank you," the lady said. "I really appreciate it."

"No problem." Katie waved her off.

"You're a sweetheart, you know that?" She eyed Katie. "Are you from around here? You don't look familiar."

Ugh. Another small town, where everybody knew everybody.

As the clerk slowly put the lady's purchases into a paper bag, Katie glanced out the window. Zach must be going crazy wondering what was taking so long.

"No," Katie said. "Just visiting."

"Well, you have a wonderful time," the lady said, taking her bag from the clerk. She turned toward the door.

"Thanks," Katie stepped up to the counter. "Just the gas. Pumps six and seven."

He rang it up. "One hundred ninety-six, even. You prepaid two hundred forty."

He opened the till and began counting back her change. Still at the speed of mud.

She clutched the money and headed for the door.

And as she opened it, she heard a siren in the distance.

Evan heard a wailing siren at the same moment as he glanced in his mirror and saw the approaching ambulance. He slowed and moved over into a right-hand lane to let it go by.

Before he moved back into his original lane, Elizabeth pulled into it and sped past him.

At least she wouldn't be riding his bumper anymore.

Maybe she was in a real big hurry to get to Canada.

Whatever. It was good to have her in front, anyway, because it was easier to see her and make sure she was okay. When she was behind him, she might have pulled over for a flat tire or something, and he might not have noticed she wasn't back there.

Nah – he'd have noticed. He'd be missing the vehicle attached to his bumper.

Ahead, brake lights started coming on, and Evan touched his own to disengage the cruise control. Soon, traffic in all the lanes slowed. Then slowed again. Finally, they were barely going ten miles per hour.

That ambulance must have been going to a wreck.

With any luck, it was only blocking one or two lanes. Otherwise, this delay could take a long time – especially if there'd been a fatality.

Mom sat up straight and leaned toward the windshield, looking at all the traffic.

"Seems like a lot of people for a Sunday evening," she said.

"It's not a normal Sunday." Evan braked again, making a point of leaving extra space between his truck and Elizabeth's car.

He glanced over his right shoulder. Dad's eyes were closed. He appeared to be napping in the back seat.

How he'd gotten comfortable enough to do that, Evan couldn't imagine. But Dad had an amazing ability to fall asleep anywhere, almost instantly, and wake up half an hour later feeling bright eyed and bushy tailed.

Evan didn't inherit that gift. He usually couldn't fall asleep unless he was perfectly comfortable or totally exhausted. Which explained the frequent bags under his eyes.

Traffic slowed again, and both the center lane and the right lane came to a complete stop.

Elizabeth, directly ahead of him in the center lane, signaled to move into the left hand lane.

Yeah, good luck with that. Drivers in that lane were bumper to bumper, traveling maybe ten miles an hour. They wouldn't be letting anyone in.

Not even a knockout beauty like Elizabeth.

If she were driving a convertible, with the top down so she was visible, then maybe. Otherwise, nope.

But suddenly, her car lurched forward. A small space had opened in the left-hand lane, and she was gunning for it. The Audi snaked into the slot, and Elizabeth was on her way.

Without them.

Evan shook his head. Great. This was just great.

He flicked on his turn signal to follow her, knowing it was an exercise in futility. There was no way he was going to be able to get the pickup into that packed lane of vehicles.

Soon, Elizabeth would be far ahead, and they'd have no way to communicate so they could re-connect. She'd be on her own, and he'd feel responsible for her.

And it was beginning to get dark.

Alana slipped down the hall to the ladies' room. She just needed a few minutes of silence. A moment away from the chaos swirling in the PEOC.

She stepped to the mirror and applied fresh lipstick. It helped brighten her face, but did nothing to mask the fatigue evident in her eyes.

For the better part of two days, she hadn't eaten well, barely slept, and consumed far too much coffee. She'd continue drinking the coffee, too – at this point, she needed the caffeine to function.

She sighed and smoothed her black curls.

Maybe tonight she'd get some sleep.

No. Tonight she'd definitely get a lot of sleep. She had to – another night like last night would leave her worthless tomorrow. And tomorrow, the markets – ugh! Tomorrow would have to wait.

Today was bad enough.

Another sigh, this one deeper than the one before. It seemed to emanate from the bottom of her psyche.

This life was aging her before her time. Were those wrinkles in her forehead?

She leaned toward the mirror. Yep. And tiny lines were forming at the corners of her mouth, too.

Frown lines? Smile wrinkles?

Did it matter? Her skin had always been smooth and flawless. She needed more sleep. And hydration.

She stretched her back, rolled her shoulders, and left the restroom. At the end of the hall, a set of doors led into the PEOC, and she forced her feet to move toward them.

A fleeting image of her turning around and running the opposite way flashed through her mind.

If only.

If only she could do that.

But no. She strode toward the doors, pushed through them, and braced herself.

Whatever happened next, she'd be here to help Basilia with it. That was her job. Her responsibility.

And what Basilia really needed her to do, was deal with the California crisis, including capturing Zachary Nelson.

So that's what she would focus on. She couldn't put out the conflagration destroying the state. Nobody could. Those fires would burn until they ran out of fuel.

But they could catch a suspect. And they would.

If it was the last thing she did.

CHAPTER TWENTY-SEVEN

As the sound of sirens filled her ears, Katie ran to the pickup. Zach pulled away from the pumps and drove toward the highway. She jumped in the truck and followed him.

The sirens grew louder.

Oh, Lord – please!

The motorhome lumbered onto the highway, headed west. Moments later, Katie pulled out behind it.

As she gripped the steering wheel, tears filled her eyes.

Had they come this far, only to be snatched up outside tiny Lakeview, Oregon? The place was hardly even on the map!

Obviously, that clerk in the gas station had recognized Katie and called them in. He'd been a good actor – he'd never made any obvious sign that he was onto her. Pretty slick, for somebody so young.

As they reached the end of town and began picking up speed, Katie saw lights behind her.

They were quite a distance back, though, and there were several vehicles between the cops and her. She pressed the gas pedal. The tank was full. Might as well use some of it!

She longed to talk to Zach. They might only have a couple of minutes of freedom left. She reached for the walkie, but forced herself to put it down.

Anything she said, the police would be able to pick up on their radios. They were well within the little walkie's broadcast distance.

She blinked, and tears fell on her cheeks.

Oh, Lord.

Cars behind her began pulling over to let the cops go past.

This was it.

Katie brushed away her tears and switched on her turn signal, letting off the gas and pulling over toward the highway's shoulder. Ahead of her, the motorhome was doing the same.

Dear Jesus. Help.

In her side mirror, she watched as the police car raced toward them. She choked on her tears.

What would happen to Timothy? And Duke?

That big ole dog wouldn't take kindly to anyone he viewed as hostile. Or a threat.

Would they shoot her dog?

Fresh tears blurred her vision. Hopefully, Timothy could stay with his grandparents. In Baltimore or Galloway or wherever they were.

How would she get word to them, though?

She watched the cop car approaching. And saw another one not far behind it.

Looking in the makeup mirror, she wiped away streaking mascara. No need to look like a crying crazy. It'd just scare Timothy, who no doubt would freak out anyway.

She pulled in a deep breath and rolled down her window.

But the cop car didn't stop behind her. It rolled on past, its siren shrieking.

When it didn't stop behind Zach, either, Katie couldn't believe her eyes.

What?!

The second cop car came screaming by, and Katie saw a third coming, as well. But wait, the third one was different. Bigger.

As it went by, she saw paramedic insignia on the doors of the white SUV.

She sat dumbfounded, as the procession wailed on up the highway. It took a minute before she could really believe they were undiscovered.

Thank you, Lord. She turned on her signal to return to the traffic lanes. As she looked in her mirror, she saw another vehicle with flashing lights.

An ambulance.

She waited until it had passed, then slowly pulled back onto the highway. Zach moved out ahead of her.

Again, she swiped at her tears and tried to settle her nerves.

They really needed to find a place to hide. Soon.

She couldn't take much more of this.

Evan scanned the left-hand lane, looking for a chance to move over and try to catch up to Elizabeth. Who was probably a half-mile ahead by now.

His own lane inched forward, but he hung back, creating enough room to maneuver the pickup forward and to the left... if he ever got a chance.

What had she been thinking, anyway, taking off like that?

Did she imagine his truck was as nimble as her little sedan?

It wasn't.

Or did she think he was driving too cautiously or slow?

That could explain her tailgating, then overtaking him in the middle lane.

Maybe she didn't like following behind a larger vehicle. It limited her field of vision. If that were the case, though, she could have just allowed a normal amount of space between her vehicle and his, instead of plastering her car to his bumper.

Perhaps she didn't care whether she traveled with his family or alone. Or she'd decided to ditch them.

If so, that was pretty dumb, given the current state of events in the country.

Traveling solo might become dangerous tonight.

"I just sent your brother a text," Mom said, looking up from her cell phone.

He glanced over at her. "I'm sure he's gotten rid of his phone by now."

"I guess. But maybe he can get another phone and retrieve his texts later." She glanced around at the barely moving traffic. "Where's Elizabeth? I thought she was in front of us."

"She was. She is. Somewhere."

Mom turned to look straight at him. "You lost her? How could you do that?"

"It's the other way around. She lost us," Evan said. "She swerved into the left hand lane, which as you can see, is actually still moving."

"Well, get over there."

"Easier said than done. I've been trying."

"Just go for it. They'll let you in, once you start into their lane."

He glanced over at her. "I'm not going to get into a wreck, just to catch up to Elizabeth."

"You lost Elizabeth?" Dad's groggy voice came from behind him. He must have just woken up.

Great. Evan rolled his eyes. Here we go again.

Now it's Dad's turn.

As Alana stepped into the PEOC, the president was speaking in her loud authority voice.

"Listen up, people!"

The room hushed almost instantly.

"We need to talk about martial law. And I want lots of input from all of you," Basilia's gaze drifted to Alana and stopped there. "We've got people coming out of the blast zone, and they're covered in radioactive dust and ash. It's falling off everywhere, contaminating everything. Cars, busses, sidewalks, hospitals, restaurants – you name it."

She glanced at the defense secretary.

"Some of the cabinet members want to impose martial law on the whole region, to halt the spread of this human-carried radioactive contamination." The president, standing behind her black leather chair, rested her hands on the backrest. "The military is mobilizing at this moment to begin setting up checkpoints and road blocks. I need to know if any of you have concerns that we should address."

For a moment, no one spoke.

Alana drew a slow breath. Martial law was a big deal. She didn't know the last time it'd been imposed – perhaps not in her entire lifetime.

Then again, nothing like this attack had ever happened before, either.

No U.S. city had ever suffered a nuclear incident like this. There had been the partial meltdown of the nuclear reactor at Three Mile Island, but that was before she was born. It was an accident, not a terrorist attack. And the remaining reactor there had been decommissioned in 2019.

In her mind, the biggest concern with martial law might be lawsuits afterward. She glanced at the attorney general to see if he was going to say anything. He was studying the coffee in his cup.

Was that because he was deep in thought? Or because he wasn't sure what to say?

"Nobody?" Basilia prompted. "None of you have any concerns about imposing martial law in New York? We're going to suspend the population's civil rights, constitutional liberties and freedoms, and nobody here wants to talk about it?"

Finally, the attorney general cleared his throat.

"I think you've summed it up pretty well," he said. "The residents who've just survived this horrific attack are now going to be subject to extreme inconvenience, to spare people outside the fallout area from possible contamination."

"Extreme inconvenience?" Alana echoed. "You know it's so much worse than that! They're likely to spend the next days and weeks dying of radiation poisoning. A slow, tortured death!"

She hadn't meant to get involved in a debate, but the AG's mischaracterization of the reality of the situation galled her.

Inconvenience? It was more like a death sentence.

CHAPTER TWENTY-EIGHT

Katie followed Zach through the semi-arid, sparsely populated region of southern Oregon. They continued west as the sun lowered in the sky. Eventually they descended into another valley, this one broader and more agricultural than the last.

The highway wove its away through irrigated farms tilled from the dry soil. And soon a city spread out before them. Or a significant town, at least. The signs said it was Klamath Falls.

Katie bit her lip. She should stop somewhere and get hair dye.

But the thought of stopping – of getting out of this pickup again, where the public could see and recognize her – filled her with dread.

It was a big risk.

On the other hand, so was continuing on the way they were, looking exactly like they did in the images all over TV and the internet.

Which was riskier?

She sighed.

As she approached town, she drove by a golf course and was astonished to see golfers out on the green.

What were they thinking?!

Their neighbors to the south, in California, were burning to death! And their fellow citizens in New York had been incinerated!

And these people were out golfing?

She'd drifted to the shoulder of the road as she gawked at them, and now she had to swerve to get back in her lane.

Good job, Kate. Get in a stupid wreck because you're distracted. That'd be great.

But those golfers! Ugh!

She focused her attention ahead, watching for a store that might carry hair color. Picking up the walkie talkie, she pressed the transmit button.

"Runner, you there?"

Static. Maybe he didn't have his radio turned on. Or maybe it'd been on too long, and the batteries were dead.

"Runner?"

"Go ahead." His voice crackled.

"I need to stop at a store."

"What for?"

She didn't want to say it was for hair dye. Anybody could be listening in, and... you just never know.

"Some stuff for my hair," she said.

"Where do you want to go?"

"Grocery store or Walmart or something."

"I'll watch for one," he said.

Good enough. Maybe they'd be lucky, and he wouldn't find a store along this route. She'd be just as happy to not take the risk.

They'd taken a lot of those today, and she felt like they were running out of luck.

But they hadn't gone two more blocks before his turn signal came on for a right-hand turn. And she saw the sign for a chain store.

Great.

She followed him into the parking lot, and they parked toward the rear, away from the store's main entrance.

Rather than go directly inside, she walked to the motorhome and climbed into the passenger seat.

"How're you holding up?" Zach studied her with tired eyes. He reached over and squeezed her shoulder.

"I'm hanging in there," she said. "I nearly had a heart attack when those cops came screaming up behind us."

"You and me both. I looked back at Timothy and thought –" his voice cracked, and he didn't finish the sentence.

Katie turned around to see their son. He'd dozed off in his car seat again. She turned back to her husband and spoke in a hushed voice.

"I'm scared to go in there."

"You don't have to," he said. "We can just get back on the road and keep going."

"Yeah, but –" she pressed her fingers against her lips. "If we don't change our look, somebody is going to recognize us. It's just a matter of time."

"Or somebody could recognize you if you go in there," Zach said, looking at the store.

"I know!" She fell silent and watched shoppers coming out of the building. "What should I do?"

He took her hand. His felt strong and warm. She turned her eyes to his.

"I think it's okay," he said.

"I do, too." But she didn't move. She didn't want to let go of his hand.

Finally, she sighed.

"Okay. I'm going."

Instead of releasing her hand, he pulled her toward him, his deep blue eyes fixed on her. His other hand slid behind her head as he moved in for a kiss.

Eventually, Evan's lane began moving at an almost-reasonable speed. Finding Elizabeth seemed unlikely, especially as night closed in. Soon, it would be difficult to make out much more than headlights and taillights. He might end up four vehicles behind her, and not even realize it.

After he went past the right-lane wreck that had caused the traffic jam in the first place, he poured on the gas and moved into the left lane.

There didn't seem to be a lot of police patrolling the freeway this evening.

Perhaps they were dealing with more serious problems. Or maybe they were calling in sick, so they could take care of their own families.

In any event, getting a speeding ticket was the least of his concerns. He didn't know if he'd be in the country to pay it when the due date arrived, or if the courthouse would even still be hearing cases three weeks from now.

And judging by the way traffic was moving, nobody else was too concerned about tickets, either.

The fast lane was traveling at least 15 miles per hour over the posted speed limit.

He was making good time, when he spotted a blue Audi in the center lane, not too far ahead.

Could it be Elizabeth?

Suddenly, he felt energized. He'd pretty much given up on finding her unless the cell phones started working again.

He squinted and stared through the deepening dusk.

It did look like her car!

Relief and lightness lifted his chest.

A grin pulled at the corners of his mouth. That had to be her!

Maybe he was an idiot. He should probably be mad at her for taking off like that. But in reality, he was thrilled to find her.

He couldn't remember the last time he'd been so happy to see someone.

"I think calling it a death sentence is a little harsh," the attorney general said, giving Alana a pointed look. "I'm sure the military will be setting up decontamination units."

"Of course," the secretary of defense responded. "Residents inside the quarantine area will be allowed to leave, as soon as we've deconned them."

"How many can you process?" Basilia looked at him. "In say, an hour?"

"When we're fully set up, we can decontaminate one hundred people per hour."

"But that's fewer than three thousand per day!" Alana protested. "Meanwhile, all the others who've survived so far will have to remain in a radioactive area. Nearly everyone will get sick and die."

The president touched her earlobe. She looked at the military boss. "She's right. We need to get people out of there. Can't you transport them outside the radioactive zone, contain them somewhere and decontaminate them?"

He shook his head.

"No. That just creates the same problem we have now – moving contaminated people spreads contamination. If we put them in trucks, trains or busses, they'll contaminate those units, as well as the area they travel through."

He paused. "Look, I know this is awful. But there's only so much we can do. We're going to lose a lot of the population, but we'll save as many as we can."

"So." Basilia's gaze roamed the room. "Your plan is to set up roadblocks, fencing or whatever, to keep the contaminated population inside the fallout zone."

"Until we can process them out, yes."

"Only a couple thousand per day," Alana reiterated.

"Approximately," the defense secretary hedged.

"They might revolt," Alana said.

"Most of New York is pretty well disarmed," he pointed out. "We can handle a few misguided individuals."

"And outside of New York?" she persisted. "What if their family members rise up? Demand you let them out to get medical help and humanitarian assistance?"

"Seriously?" He leveled his gaze at her, then turned to the president. "Nobody is going to 'rise up,' Madam President. Or not more than a handful here or there. Nothing local law enforcement can't deal with. They're well equipped for that kind of thing."

Alana's face grew warm. He was probably right, though. Americans had been carefully conditioned to be soft and compliant. And for two decades, the military had been supplying local LEOs with armored personnel carriers and other military gear.

Resistance would be futile.

CHAPTER TWENTY-NINE

Katie stepped out of the motorhome and drew a deep breath as she turned apprehensively toward the front of the store.

Her mouth instantly dried like the desert she'd driven through earlier.

A warm breeze teased her hair as she pressed her purse against side, lowered the brim of her hat, and headed toward the doors. She reminded herself to keep her chin down to avoid security cameras.

As she entered, she grabbed a hand basket, then glanced toward the checkout lanes, hoping to see some self-checkouts.

No such luck. She'd have to deal with a cashier.

Keeping her sunglasses on, she began looking for the area where she'd find hair products. She didn't want to ask anybody for help or directions.

Didn't want anyone to look at her for any reason, actually.

After a couple of minutes, she located the cosmetics and hair care.

Now, what to get? With her light brown hair, she could easily go darker or redder. She definitely didn't want any crazy colors.

The idea was to disguise herself and blend in, not draw any attention. So not too red, either. Black, maybe?

It'd look unnatural with her lighter skin tone, but it wasn't any shade of her natural brown, either.

She huffed out a sigh.

"Need some help?"

Until she spoke, Katie hadn't noticed the clerk approaching behind her.

"No." Katie glanced at her, then quickly away. "Thanks. I'm fine."

"Sure. Let me know if you need anything." She moved on down the aisle, placing stock on the shelves.

Katie grabbed a dark brown dye for Zach. It was easy to pick something for him. Anything but blond.

Then she grabbed a rich dark mahogany color with reddish tones for herself. And two boxes of black, just in case.

Maybe it was kind of odd to just buy four boxes of assorted hair dye. So on the way to the registers, she grabbed a tube of toothpaste, a bar of soap, and a loofa. Perhaps that was ridiculous.

She could just imagine being arrested, and her purchases winding up in the reports. Hair dye and a loofa.

Keeping her chin down as she approached the checkout lanes, she picked the one that seemed shortest. It had three people ahead of her.

"We're only taking cash," the clerk barked as she joined the line.

Katie nodded.

The man directly ahead of her was an older gentleman, probably in his seventies, wearing a navy polo shirt and khaki shorts. He smiled at her.

"It's because of New York," he said. "The banks, you know."

She nodded tightly. Really didn't want to get pulled into a conversation. She feigned interest in the magazine rack, then saw the candy bars.

She reached for the dark chocolate with almonds.

"That's my favorite, too," the man said.

Katie gave him a weak smile and turned back to the magazines, lifting one from the rack and flipping it open.

This line did not seem to be moving at all. From the corner of her eye, she saw the clerk trying to manually enter a code for a pink baby onesie.

Great. This could take forever!

She turned around, checking out the other lines. They seemed to be moving at the speed of snails, too.

As she turned back, her basket bumped into someone who'd just joined her line.

"Oh! I'm sorry," Katie said. She glanced at the newcomer.

Her breath stalled in her throat. It was a very good looking, dark-haired young man.

And he was wearing the uniform of a sheriff's deputy.

Evan drew alongside Elizabeth's car.

"Mom, give her a wave," he said.

Mom waved frantically, with both hands. Evan cringed.

"She saw me!" Mom looked his way, grinning. She turned back and gave Elizabeth another wave.

"Okay, great." He let traffic pull him forward.

Moments later, Elizabeth swung into his lane behind the pickup.

And promptly plastered herself on his bumper.

Evan shook his head as he glanced in his mirror. But he wouldn't let this get to him. At least he'd found her, and she was safe back there. As long as she didn't crash into him or something.

Traffic was moving nearly 20 m.p.h. over the speed limit in the fast lane now, and Evan kept up with it. Soon, he'd pull off at a gas station to fill up, but he'd wait until Mom or Dad needed a bathroom break.

For now, they were making good time, and he wanted to get as many miles under the wheels as he could.

As dusk gave way to dark, though, his concerns grew.

They'd be pulling off the freeway at night, at an unfamiliar location that might not be particularly safe. Even places that were ordinarily safe during the day could be worse and night.

And this weekend, any place held the potential to be dangerous, given the volatility of the population's reactions to the national crises.

He tried not to worry about it.

Traveling at night carried that risk, but waiting to travel until morning had seemed like a worse choice. They'd discussed their options and made a decision.

Hopefully, it was the right one.

They'd all have to keep their eyes open and their guard up.

At least there were four of them. Safety in numbers, and all that.

And Elizabeth had the sense to wait for them in the center lane until he could catch up with her. Perhaps she'd had concerns of her own as the world darkened around them all.

———

Alana glanced at the president, who was looking straight at her.

"Thank you, Alana. That was the kind of debate I was looking for," she said.

What, the kind where Alana made a fool of herself?

Well, at least Basilia was happy. She probably just wanted to have a roundtable discussion of the matter so later she could say it was thoroughly deliberated by her cabinet. Which is hardly what had transpired, but who would know?

"Okay, people – martial law is happening," the president

announced. "My press secretary and her team will be working on talking points and a press release."

She glanced at the director of Homeland Security and added, "On the bright side, since cell phones aren't working in that region, we won't have to worry about horrific images and protests coming out of there on social media."

Alana bit her lip so she wouldn't say what she was thinking. Cell phones and social media were down, sure, but there were plenty of horrific images all over television and the internet already.

With many more to come, for days and weeks in the future.

Since it was obvious the meeting on martial law had ended, she turned her thoughts back to her main objective for the day – dealing with California and Zachary James Nelson. Surely the FBI director had some news for her by now. He was standing in the far corner, talking with the transportation secretary.

She made her way over to him.

His shifty eyes glanced her way, then back to the secretary as he finished his sentence. Then he turned to her.

"An update?" She didn't need to tell him for what. He knew.

"Right." He took a sip of his coffee. "Unfortunately, I don't have one yet."

Not good enough! She narrowed her eyes.

"You mean to say absolutely nothing has come to light since we last spoke?" She glanced at her watch. "Like, an hour ago?"

"What I mean is, we haven't caught him yet."

"So you don't know where he is," she countered.

"We know where he was, and we're searching."

"It's possible, then, that he evaded you and left town." She crossed her arms. "Have you gotten reports of sightings anywhere else in that region?"

He actually chuckled.

"Sure! We're getting thousands of reports of sightings of Mr. Nelson, all across the country! Somebody even saw him boarding an airplane in Las Vegas thirty minutes ago, which is shocking because all commercial aircraft is grounded."

His flat eyes looked bored.

"Look, I'll let you know when we pick him up. Or shoot him down, whichever comes first."

CHAPTER THIRTY

Katie tried to resist the urge to drop her basket and run.

"No worries," the deputy said. His gaze turned to the contents of her basket, then back to her eyes. Or sunglasses, actually.

If she ran, he'd be sure to stop her.

If she stayed here, he'd be sure to recognize her.

She looked at her basket. Lots of hair dye.

Her mouth felt like dried plaster. As her heart hammered her ribs, she swallowed and turned to face the clerk.

She couldn't stay here!

She couldn't run!

Lord, help! What do I do?

Wait.

Wait? For what?

Her pulse drummed her ears. Heat crept into her cheeks.

Great! If she didn't look suspicious before, she sure did now. With a red face and everything.

Behind her, the deputy began talking quietly. Katie turned slightly and glanced at him. He held his cell phone to his ear, listening.

Was he calling for backup?

"No, man, I forgot the peanut butter!" he said.

Was that some kind of code word? Or was he really talking about peanut butter?

"You like crunchy, right?"

Either that was an especially weird code, or he actually was talking about peanut butter.

"Okay." He ended the call, put the phone in his pocket, and got out of line. Presumably headed for the grocery section.

Go. Now.

The voice in her head was insistent. Katie backed away from the line, then turned and started for the doors. Still holding the shopping basket.

She set it down at the end of an aisle and straightened up, trying to look nonchalant. Then she beelined for the exit.

They'd have to do without the hair dye.

Stepping out the doors, she felt like a prisoner must feel when he escapes.

Fresh air! Freedom!

She turned toward the motorhome, at the far end of the parking lot. Their pickup was parked beside it.

And a few spaces away, two police cars were parked side-by-side. The drivers' doors were aligned together, and their windows were down so the drivers could talk.

Katie stopped.

She couldn't walk over there!

It'd draw attention to her. And Zach. Who was probably hiding in the motorhome right now, praying those guys would leave.

But she couldn't just stand here in front of the store.

Pretty soon, that deputy would be coming out. He'd remember her and her hair dye, and he'd notice she wasn't holding her purchases. All his suspicions would add up to one big problem for her.

She had to get to the pickup and get out of here. Forcing one foot to follow the other, she swallowed her fears as she drew nearer to the police cars.

They were parked closer to the pickup than the motorhome. So Zach was about five parking spaces from the officers. Close enough for easy recognition, if they saw him.

Maybe they wouldn't look at her. Wouldn't notice she wasn't carrying any shopping bags. One of them was faced away from her, but she'd have to walk right in front of the other one.

She sucked dry air into desperate lungs.

Kept her chin up. Tried to look casual.

Tried to be invisible.

Her heart beat like a drummer on drugs. What if she had a heart attack and collapsed right here on the hot pavement?

She pushed on, kept walking. She'd pass by them in just a moment. If she didn't die from stress and panic.

She tried to relax her shoulders and her stride as she passed in front of one of the police cars. She turned her eyes to watch them as she walked.

The officer facing her glanced toward her. Then back at his buddy in the other car. Then back again at her.

He adjusted his sunglasses.

Did he recognize her?

Or was he checking her out?

She swallowed past a dry lump in her throat. A few more seconds, and she'd climb into the cab of the pickup. She could see herself getting in, turning the key, putting on her seatbelt, and driving out of the parking lot.

It looked so easy in her imagination.

But a million things could go wrong before that happened.

Or one big thing – being recognized.

An eternity seemed to pass before she reached the driver's door and opened it. She climbed inside. Put on her seat belt.

Looked for Zach in the RV beside her. Didn't see him, but he might be watching her through the blinds in the coach windows.

She turned on the engine. Glanced toward the police cars. She wasn't able to clearly see the officers now, but they hadn't opened their doors or anything. That must be a good sign.

Looking back at the RV, she still didn't see Zach.

Should she wait until he got into the driver's seat?

Or should she just drive off?

The longer she sat here with her engine idling, the more likely she'd be to draw the officers' attention. She'd have to move out.

Hopefully, Zach had noticed everything that was going on, and would follow her. She didn't dare use the radio to communicate with him.

She eased the pickup into gear and backed out of her space. Slowly, she drove toward the exit, checking her mirrors constantly to see if Zach or the police cars were in motion.

None of them moved.

Maybe Zach had been in the bathroom!

Maybe he had no idea the police were parked close to him, or that Katie had returned from the store and had to drive away.

If she hesitated about leaving the parking lot, the police might notice.

If she drove out without Zach – her heart thumped – would he be able to find her?

How?

When?

A grey car drove up behind her pickup. She had to make a decision quickly. Pull away from the exit and wait for Zach, or go ahead and leave the parking lot alone?

Stopping and waiting would attract attention.

She gave the truck some gas and moved forward to the stop sign. When traffic thinned, she turned right, continuing the same way she and Zach had been traveling, and immediately began looking for a place to pull over and wait for him.

Parking was prohibited along the curb, so she drove another

block and turned in at a tiny strip mall. She parked where she could best watch approaching traffic.

Eventually, she'd see Zach coming, and would rejoin him on the road.

Unless he was caught.

Evan signaled a lane change and started working his way right, toward the upcoming off ramp. He didn't have to worry about Elizabeth following him.

Predictably, she stayed right on his bumper.

Once off the freeway, he turned right at the first intersection and headed for the nearest gas station.

Huge cardboard signs announced that they were only taking cash, which perhaps explained why there weren't long lines. That and the fuel prices on the reader board, which were approximately double what he'd paid earlier in the day.

The cash issue was soon going to be a problem. He'd gotten some cash from the ATM, and Mom had, too... but not enough to repeatedly refuel at these kinds of prices.

He pulled up to a pump, saw Elizabeth drive to a pump a couple of fuel islands farther down, and then headed inside to prepay.

Ordinarily, it wouldn't cost a whole lot to top off, but with these prices... he removed eighty dollars from his wallet and handed it to the clerk.

"Pump nine, please."

The clerk counted the bills. "Eighty. Go ahead."

Elizabeth was entering as he was leaving, so he held the door open for her. He opened his mouth to say something about her tailgating, but she gave him such a disarming smile, his words evaporated from his mind before he spoke them.

Instead, he smiled like a smitten schoolboy.

Back at the truck, Mom and Dad were nowhere to be seen. Headed off to the restrooms, no doubt.

He was still smiling like an idiot as he began fueling the pickup. Seeing his giddy reflection in his windows, he erased the goofy grin and tried to look cool and collected.

It'd been a long time since a woman had such an effect on him. It felt good. Except when he realized he was acting like a doofus.

He glanced back to the store. Elizabeth was just exiting, and some tall, broad-shouldered guy was holding the door for her. She gave him the same dazzling smile she'd given Evan.

The same one she'd apparently give anybody.

Well, at least she wasn't snooty. She seemed genuinely nice – not like those girls who knew they were hot and expected everybody to acknowledge it and treat them like little queens.

He realized he was staring when she began pumping fuel and glanced his direction.

And like a teenager, he looked away too quickly, totally giving himself away.

As Alana stood speaking with Director Chalmers, one of his aides walked up. He stopped at the FBI director's elbow and whispered something in his ear.

"It's okay, Rick," the director said. "I'm sure the vice president would be interested in your update."

The young man glanced her way. "Of course. We've been getting reports of possible sightings of the California suspect in southern Oregon."

"How far from that little town in Nevada?" Alana focused on Director Chalmers. "Winnemucca. Where you were sure you had him pinned down?"

"We never had him pinned down," Chalmers said. "We knew he was there because he tripped the license plate readers."

"How far?" Alana directed her question to his aide.

"More than one hundred miles, ma'am."

She hated that word, ma'am. But decided to ignore it.

"In the amount of time that has passed, he could have driven there." She turned her eyes on the director. "Would he have gone through another license plate reader?"

Chalmers didn't answer, but looked to his aide.

"No," the young man said. "It's a small highway, not an interstate. I checked, and it doesn't have the cameras."

"So." Alana turned her glare on the director. "He got away from you."

"We don't know that. He could be laying low in Nevada, right where we're looking for him."

"I want follow up in Oregon," she ordered. "Interview these people. See what they saw."

"We're already doing that, of course," the aide said.

Alana straightened her spine. She looked pointedly at both men.

"Until this issue is resolved, I want real-time updates. Every fifteen minutes. No excuses."

She turned from them and joined her chief of staff and national security advisor, who had taken some time to rest. Jason set down the cookie he was eating. Mae looked prim and composed, though tension wrinkled her brow.

"I need the two of you to handle most of the California fire follow up," she said. "Except anything to do with the suspect. I'm focusing totally on that until we arrest him, so send any new leads on him straight to me. Just give me fire updates every hour, so I can keep the president informed."

"Sure thing, Boss," Jason said.

"We're on it," Mae agreed.

CHAPTER THIRTY-ONE

Katie fought anxiety as she waited, and waited, and waited for Zach. She bit her lip and prayed for him. Time ticked by on the dash clock.

Five minutes. Ten. Fifteen.

He'd been arrested.

She should go back and get their son and dog. But she'd be arrested then, too, as an accomplice.

On the other hand, if Zach was arrested and Timothy was turned over to CPS, she might as well be arrested. At least then, she'd have a possibility of posting bail and getting their son back. And Duke the Dog.

If she ran after Zach was arrested, she wouldn't have any opportunities to rescue Tim and Duke.

The clock showed she'd been waiting for seventeen minutes.

Might as well go back and face the music.

Her heart felt like lead as she pulled out of the strip mall parking lot and headed back to the store. But as she signaled her turn into the entrance, she saw the motorhome lumbering toward the exit.

As Zach approached, he was waving wildly at her, then shaking his head, and motioning for her to drive on by.

She checked her mirrors to see if she could get out of the turn lane and back into regular traffic. It looked impossible. Cars were backing up behind her, and there wasn't any room between vehicles in the traffic lane.

As Zach began to pull into the opposite lane of traffic, she gave him a helpless shrug. She'd have to turn in, but she could turn right around in the parking lot, and then catch up to him.

He shook his head one more time, then moved out of her view. She pulled into the parking lot. And quickly saw why he didn't want her to turn in there.

Both police cars, and the sheriff's deputy, were on their way out. In just a moment, she'd have to drive right by all of them at slow speeds.

They'd no doubt been seeing her face on internet and news feeds all day, and they'd seen her in person in the past thirty minutes. Between the three of them, the likelihood of recognition was astronomical.

As she approached the first one, she tilted her chin and turned her head like she was adjusting her radio. She averted her eyes and maintained that position as she passed the other two.

Then she cruised slowly up a parking lane toward the front of the store, watching her mirrors.

All their brake lights came on.

But of course they had to stop before leaving the parking lot. The first one exited, and Katie began to breathe again. The second one pulled out, then the third.

Thank God!

She drove around the end of the parking lane and started back toward the street. The police cars disappeared from view – two had gone left, and one had gone right. She'd have to keep her eyes peeled for that one, as it might pull off at some point along her eventual route.

Now, she just needed to find her family again.

Before that officer found them all.

She exited the parking lot again, and started down the street. It shouldn't be too hard to find Zach. There weren't a lot of good places to pull a motorhome off this road.

Maybe he didn't pull off, though.

Maybe, after getting away from those officers, he decided not to risk another stop, and just continue on through town. If he'd done that, she should be able to find him, if they both stayed on this highway.

Uncertain, she slowed at each intersection and checked up and down the cross streets.

He could have gone anywhere, after all.

She had no idea where he was.

Block after block rolled by as Katie looked for her family. More than once, she reached for the walkie talkie, then set it down again.

Maybe it was fine to broadcast over the radio waves, but she wasn't confident of that. It felt so risky.

Better to keep looking for now, and pray.

So she prayed and drove and looked up each side street.

It wasn't like he'd actually vanished, after all. They'd find each other sooner or later. But she'd prefer it to be sooner. Like right this minute!

She thought she was on Route 39, but maybe it was Sixth Street, when she suddenly saw the motorhome. It was parked on the side street just ahead, and began pulling forward to enter her lane. Relief relaxed her tight shoulders and chest as she slowed to let him in ahead of her.

Together again! She breathed a grateful thanks to her creator.

Zach signaled a turn onto a cross street that would take them south. He was the one with the maps, so hopefully he knew where they were going. It was a good thing he'd pulled over and waited for her where he did – she would have stayed on the main road, which curved north.

Finding each other would have been extremely difficult then, especially once they exceeded the short range of their walkie talkies!

That thought chilled her.

From now on, they could never afford to be separated by more than a mile, unless they had made plans to meet up in a specified location. Without cell phones or functional radios, they'd never be able to communicate to find one another.

Maybe they should ditch the pickup, and all travel together in the RV. Then they'd never lose each other.

The moment that idea crossed her mind, she realized how stupid it sounded. They'd brought the pickup for a reason. When they'd evacuated their home, they'd loaded this F-150 up with their most precious and important belongings.

And since there was a strong probability they'd never be able to return to their home in California, which had probably burned already, she was grateful they'd been able to save so many things – wedding and baby albums, important files and documents, camping gear and clothing, money and jewelry. And much more. As much as they could cram into the pickup truck.

Very few Californians had escaped with their lives, much less with any possessions.

Although it didn't feel like it at the moment, she and Zach were blessed.

She'd try to keep that in mind as they ran for their lives.

After a few minutes, the road they were on dumped its traffic onto a highway running east and west. The sign said something about a South Side Bypass. Maybe if they'd found this road when they first came into town, they wouldn't have had all the misadventures in this city.

Zach signaled a right-hand turn to travel west, and Katie followed his lead.

The sun was dropping quickly toward the horizon as they left town.

Hopefully, they'd soon find a place to hole up for the night.

Or maybe for a week or two, if they were lucky.

She thought about how much food she had – or didn't – in the motorhome. Enough for a week, if she stretched it.

Would this be over in a week?

Not the fires, obviously, or the fallout from New York, but the crazy pursuit of her husband?

In the tumult of the first day or two of the crisis, one might somehow be able to understand how the feds thought he could be involved. He'd helped organize a massive project along the entire coast where the fires began.

But with any investigation, surely clues would point to the real perpetrators.

Then they'd drop this absurd manhunt for Zach, right?

Unless the government was far more corrupt and evil that she realized.

Evan filled his gas tank and re-entered the store to get his change, passing his parents on the way. Mom had purchased a bag of potato chips, and Dad was carrying a monster-sized soft drink.

"See you out there," he said.

As he joined the line at the checkout counter, he looked out the window. Elizabeth stood next to her car, fiddling with her cell phone. She glanced at the gas pump, then back at her phone.

Was she able to get messages or texts? Maybe she'd heard something from her dad?

A minute later, Evan had his receipt and change, and returned to the pickup. Elizabeth was just hanging up the gas pump nozzle. As she went into the store, Evan moved the pickup away from the pump so the next customer could use it.

He pulled over near the parking lot's exit and waited for her to finish her transaction and return to her car.

A bright streetlight illuminated his truck, so she should see it quickly when she came out of the store and realized he wasn't still parked at the pumps.

His phone buzzed.

A call?

He grabbed it to check.

No, but it was showing incoming texts and emails now. No voice mails, yet.

Mom suddenly yelped, then swore. Evan jumped, dropping his phone in his lap.

"WHAT?" He looked around, then focused on Elizabeth's car.

Several big, unsavory characters had accosted Elizabeth next to her Audi.

One skinny thug grabbed for the keys she held in her left hand.

Evan fumbled with his seatbelt, then reached for his door handle.

A guy reached for the big purse that hung from Elizabeth's shoulder.

Evan shoved his door open and hollered.

His feet hit the pavement at a run.

One of the thugs turned his way, a sneer filling his tattooed face. As the creeps were distracted by Evan's noisy approach, Elizabeth yanked a gun out of that big purse and pointed it straight at the nose of the nearest, biggest guy.

She steadied it with both hands.

"Shoot him! SHOOT HIM!" Evan yelled.

He was nearly to them now.

What was he going to do when he got there?

Facial expressions changed in an instant from thuggery to fear. They started stepping back, away from Elizabeth.

All except that biggest guy.

"SHOOT HIM!" Evan screamed again. "DO IT NOW!"

———

The president eased into the chair next to Alana, and crossed her long legs.

Leaning close, Basilia whispered, "I hate this."

"We all do."

"No." Her dark eyes locked onto Alana's. "I mean, I really, truly hate it. All of it."

Something in her visage looked ominous. Dark and desperate.

"I know." Alana rested her hand on her friend's armrest and held her gaze. "But this will pass. Like everything else. We'll get through it."

Basilia's brows drew together as her face tightened.

"Nothing like this has happened before. Ever." She frowned. "What if – what if we can't recover? If the country can't absorb this and bounce back?"

The same idea had been troubling Alana, but she tried not to let it show.

Maybe it was because of the things the ambassador had said. He obviously believed that the ancient scriptures indicated the country would suffer total collapse and never recover.

"If it's because of Ambassador Wilford –"

"No, that's not it," the president scoffed. "That old man is a kook!"

"Okay." Alana straightened her back and turned to face her directly. "Here's the thing – the United States is different from other countries. We're resilient. Resourceful. We stand together. We *will* get through this."

She took her friend's hand. "I promise."

The president pulled away. She looked beyond Alana.

Turning in her chair, Alana saw the Treasury Secretary approaching. He looked as grim as she'd ever seen him.

"Madam President, the Asian markets have opened," he said.

Basilia rose to her feet. "And?"

"It's worse than we expected." He picked up the remote control and pointed it at the television screen across from them. "They're in a freefall."

A large graph showing the markets filled the screen. Each line, in bright red, zig-zagged downward. Twelve percent. Thirteen percent.

As the seconds ticked by, the numbers kept falling.

Just like Alana's hopes.

CHAPTER THIRTY-TWO

The highway ran northwest, skirting the lower portion of a huge lake, then turned abruptly west, into the mountains. Katie trailed the motorhome as the sun sank lower on the horizon. Soon, they were driving through a national forest.

She began looking for a good place to pull off and spend the night.

Eventually, Zach pulled into a deserted picnic area.

Katie drove in and parked beside him. As she got out, the sound of water cascading over rocks met her. There must be a creek nearby, maybe with a little waterfall or something.

The RV door opened, and Zach came out with the dog on a leash and a boisterous boy behind them.

Duke pulled toward her, his long black tail signaling his happy greeting. She patted his broad head and big, soft ears.

Timothy wrapped his arms around her leg.

"Hey, buddy!" She ran her fingers though his silky hair.

Zach pulled her into a group hug. "Boy, was that crazy back there, or what?"

"I waited so long, I thought you'd been arrested. What happened in the parking lot?"

"I couldn't leave," he said. "Those cops were parked too close. If I'd gotten into the driver seat, they'd have made me for sure. So I waited. And waited. And waited."

"But they left after you!" Katie pointed out.

"Yeah. They finally pulled out of those parking spaces, and I figured I was good to go, so I fired up the RV and headed toward the street, hoping to find you." He pulled on Duke's leash to keep him away from an old lollipop stick on the ground. "That's when I saw that they were taking a loop through the parking lot."

"Which is why you tried to wave me off, when I was turning back in there," Katie said.

"Exactly."

"Well, I didn't get anything at the store, because there was a deputy in my checkout line," she told him. "I got out of there, beelined for the pickup, and saw the cops."

She shook her head. "It was close, Zach."

"I know." He reached for her hand, and she took Timothy's with her free hand.

Together, they walked a little ways along a trail so Duke could empty his bladder.

"We need to find a place to spend the night. Or maybe the week," Katie said. "Pretty soon, it's going to get dark."

His eyebrows tightened. He looked around the forest.

"I don't feel good here. I'd like to get closer to the coast."

"I don't think I'll feel good anywhere," she said. "Until they stop hunting us."

They started back toward the parking lot. Katie's stomach rumbled.

"We should have a bite to eat, anyway." She looked at him. "I'm sure Timothy is hungry."

"Probably not." Zach led the way to the RV and opened the door for his family. "I fed him when we stopped at that store."

"Him? Or both of you?"

He winked. "We were both hungry."

"Men!" Katie climbed into the motorhome, with Duke on her heels. "Well, I need to eat something. What did you guys have?"

"Barbequed beans." Zach pulled the door closed behind them.

"What?" Katie turned to him. "That's all?"

"We ate the whole can," he admitted. "With crackers."

"Oh, good heavens!" She gave him the stink eye as she opened a cabinet to find something for her own dinner. "We're going to have to sleep with the windows open tonight!"

Two of the thugs turned and ran as Evan approached. The biggest one raised his hands and stepped back as Elizabeth pointed the gun at his face.

Evan launched himself toward the last guy, the skinny one who'd grabbed her keys, and now held them in his hand.

As the thug turned to run, Evan slammed into his midsection.

Together, they sprawled to the pavement and the keys went flying.

Pain flashed through Evan's knee as his hands formed fists. He plowed his first punch into the guy's jaw, and the second one into his stomach.

His peripheral vision registered the big guy turning and running away. Must have believed Elizabeth was going to shoot him.

A fist smashed his eye, then one crunched into his stomach, nearly knocking the wind out of him.

As he gasped, the skinny guy scrambled to his feet. He was off and running, leaving Elizabeth's keys on the ground where they'd fallen.

Evan reached out and snatched them. He rolled to his knees, scanning for the attackers.

They disappeared into the darkness around the corner of the building.

Elizabeth slid the gun into her bag. She turned wide eyes on him.

"Are you okay?" She extended a hand to him.

He took it and stood up, feeling grit and blood in his palms. "I'm alright. You?"

She nodded.

"We need to get out of here," she said. "I don't want to wait for the cops."

"Really?" He handed over her keys. "You okay to drive?"

She looked at him like he was nuts. Like this was something that happened every day.

"Of course." She took a deep breath. "I'm sorry. I was so stupid. Not paying attention to my surroundings."

"You're blaming yourself for this?" He shook his head. "You could've been killed. Or carjacked. Where'd you get that gun, anyway?"

His parents hurried up, full of questions and concern. Elizabeth held up her hand to quiet them. She glanced around at the gawkers staring at them, who hadn't offered any help.

"I'm fine. We're okay. I just want to get out of here."

Alana pulled her gaze from the collapsing Asian stock markets on the screen, and glanced toward the president.

Basilia's jaw hung loose. Her eyes were wide. Almost wild.

The president pursed her lips. Swallowed. Frowned.

And suddenly turned to Alana.

"Make it stop!" She hissed.

The markets? How?

Not knowing what else to do, Alana scooped up the remote and changed the channel.

New images showed Americans, like zombies, trying to climb over a chain link fence guarded by men in military uniforms holding big black rifles. Behind them billowed smoke from hundreds of burning buildings, illuminated by flames.

She would have thought it was a scene from California, except for the fence and the military. No, this was New York, as the national guard was fencing in the unlucky population that had survived the first blast but would be "quarantined" until they died of radiation poisoning.

A young woman neared the top of the fence, where rolls of razor wire might prevent escape.

A bullhorn blared a warning.

The woman climbed higher. Someone in the throng below threw her a jacket, which she draped over the razor wire.

Slowly, she lifted one foot over the fence.

A battery of gunfire filled the speakers. The woman shook and lurched as she was struck.

A weird gurgle came from Alana's left.

Basilia!

Alana looked for the power button. Found it! Turned it off.

The president's face was pale as death. She reached for the back of a chair to steady herself. Then eased into it.

"They just killed that girl," she muttered. "On national television!"

Her wide eyes turned to Alana.

"We're doomed."

CHAPTER THIRTY-THREE

As they pulled out of the picnic area and back onto the highway, Katie munched on a granola bar. Not a decent meal, to be sure, but it was quick and would keep her going for now. Hopefully, Zach would find a place to camp soon.

He'd mentioned wanting to be closer to the coast. What had he meant by that? Surely he wasn't planning on driving all the way over to the ocean tonight! That was hours away.

And it'd be dark soon.

She sighed.

It'd be good to find a nice, secluded little spot to hunker down. She couldn't wait to crawl up into their sleeping loft over the cab, and close her eyes on this horrible day.

If possible, it'd almost been worse than yesterday.

And it wasn't over yet.

She felt more secure on this little rural highway through the national forest. But she knew anything could happen. They were a long way from being safe.

As she drove, she prayed. For protection. For courage. For wisdom and strength.

But that was all for herself.

Tears filled her eyes as she prayed for her man and her little boy. Oh, Lord! If you would please keep us safe. And together....

The tears dropped onto her cheeks as she blinked.

She took a sip of water. Fatigue was setting in. Which made sense, since her sleep-deprived body had been flooded so many times with adrenaline over the past two days.

When would this nightmare end?

Day darkened into night, and they passed the entrances to several campgrounds, but Zach didn't pull over. Eventually, they'd drive out of this forest.

Then where would they stay? Along some county road? In a parking lot in some town?

She was tired, and she knew she was feeling cranky, but what was he thinking?

Finally, she reached for the walkie talkie.

"Runner?"

She waited, hearing only static.

"Hey, Runner!"

"Go ahead, Mermaid." His voice was hushed. Maybe Timothy had fallen asleep.

"I'm getting tired. And we're running out of forest."

"I really don't like it here."

What was she supposed to say to that? Several possibilities entered her mind, but none of them were very nice.

"We don't have a lot of options," she finally responded.

"I know." He sounded annoyed. "We'll find something."

A few minutes later, little lights twinkled in the distance. They were approaching civilization again. And that meant suspicious people and lots of police.

Katie clenched her jaw.

How much more of this could she take?

Not much. She was sure of that.

As the twinkling lights grew closer, farms sprouted up along the road. Then rural subdivisions, followed by neighborhoods and communities. A sign indicated the city limits of White City.

They turned south, and before she knew it, there were signs for Medford.

A town large enough that she'd actually heard of it before.

What was Zach thinking?!

She radioed him again.

"Do you have a plan?" She listened to static as she released the mic button.

"Yeah. Since it's dark, I thought we'd go shopping. It won't take long, and then we can head out."

Katie gulped. The thought of going back into a store where she could be recognized terrified her. On the other hand, this might be their best opportunity.

Nobody would recognize Zach in the motorhome in the dark. And it would be easier to be anonymous in a larger town.

Maybe she could hustle in, get their stuff, and bail out of there pronto.

"Okay," she said, without any enthusiasm.

She'd have to run the gauntlet. Again.

"Let's go to a big store that has self-checkout stations."

"Sure thing."

She glanced at her gas tank gauge. They should probably top off the tanks. Who knew when they'd have another opportunity?

"Let's stop for gas, too," she said.

"You got it."

Her eyes felt dry and tired. She yawned and blinked. Not much better, but a little.

Soon, Zach was signaling a turn into a gas station.

A hand-lettered cardboard sign hung from the pumps with duct tape. It read, "Premium only. CASH only!"

Great. They'd be paying top dollar at this station. Still, it was open, and had fuel, and the pump area was poorly lit.

The motorhome rolled to a stop at a pump on the end of the

fuel line, and Katie waited as the car on the opposite side of that fuel island pulled away. She took its spot.

Zach rolled down his window as she approached.

"Did you see those prices?" His tone was incredulous.

She glanced at the pumps.

It was $8.97 for a gallon of premium!

"Highway robbery!" She turned back to him. "Should we leave?"

He shook his head. "I've been listening to the news on the radio. Gas isn't going to be available for long, so we should fill up now."

"If you say so." She glanced toward the store. "I'm going to prepay."

No one besides the cashier was inside the store, so less than a minute later, she was back. She started pumping gas into the RV, then began filling the pickup's tank.

When the truck was topped off, she hung up the nozzle and waited for the motorhome to finish fueling.

Moments later, the pump stopped. It seemed too soon for the tank to be full, so Katie tried the pump handle again. Nothing.

"That's weird," she said. "I paid for more than that!"

Zach nodded. "Maybe they just ran out of gas."

She screwed on the gas cap. "Maybe."

As Katie had been fueling the tanks, several other customers had arrived and entered the business.

Pulling her hat brim low, she wished she could wear her sunglasses into the store, but since the sun had gone down long ago, that would just draw attention.

Her face would be visible. And that was that.

At least she had enough cash to pay for these extortion fill ups. When she'd stashed money every month in their safe at home, it'd been planned for something big, like their tenth anniversary. She'd never dreamed she'd be spending it on nearly $9 gas in Oregon.

"Pray I don't get caught." Clutching her wallet, she started for the store.

———

Evan couldn't take his eyes off Elizabeth. Who was this woman? Why was she carrying that big gun in her purse? She seemed like she knew what she was doing with it, too.

She was a complete stranger he'd known nearly all his life.

People from the nearby gas pumps who'd just gawked before, now started coming toward them.

"Are you okay?" A dark-haired quarterback-type guy asked. Looking only at Elizabeth, not him.

Where'd he been when they needed help?

"We're fine." She gave him a thin smile, then looked back at Evan's parents. "Please, let's just go."

"Okay." Dad nodded, but turned to Evan. "That rear seat is a little cramped. How about if I drive the truck and you ride with Elizabeth for a while?"

"Sure." It sounded like a good idea. Evan glanced at Elizabeth. "If that's okay with you?"

"Yeah." She opened her door. "Let's get out of here."

Evan handed his keys to Dad and got in Elizabeth's passenger seat. "Nice car."

"Dad gave it to me when I graduated college." She fastened her seatbelt, then glanced at him. "It was used."

He wasn't sure why she'd told him that. Maybe so he didn't think she was a spoiled rich kid?

She followed his parents out to the street and back onto the freeway, heading north.

Now that he was here with her, and they had time to talk, he had no idea what to talk about. And his mind was still processing the incident.

If she hadn't had that gun, what would have happened? Did they intend to kidnap her, or "just" steal her car?

Elizabeth drove in silence, right on Dad's bumper.

"Have you always been a tailgater?" He asked before he thought it through.

"What?" She glanced at him, but her face indicated her thoughts were a million miles away. She looked forward and touched her brakes. "I don't like driving after dark."

"Why do you carry a gun?"

She was silent for a long moment, then spoke quietly. "For times like that."

"It's happened before?" He studied her profile in the dark vehicle. "To you?"

She swallowed, then cleared her throat.

"I don't want to talk about it."

Doomed.

Basilia's word reverberated in Alana's mind. Something about that word, and hearing the president utter it, shook her to her very core.

It admitted defeat, total loss and destruction.

"No," Alana objected. She sounded hoarse. "No, we're not."

She wasn't ready to accept that. She would never be ready.

Drawing a deep breath, she filled her lungs and bloodstream with oxygen. They'd fight this. Fight the Iranians, if that's who did it. Fight everyone.

Go down fighting.

In her peripheral vision, she saw the FBI director approaching. Had it been fifteen minutes? Did he have good news?

They certainly could use some of that!

She turned expectant eyes toward him. He looked upbeat. Definitely a positive sign!

He barely seemed to register the discouragement in her little group as he joined them.

"Good chance your fugitive's in Oregon." He glanced between Alana and the president. "Local authorities there have been interviewing witnesses who reported seeing Mr. Nelson. Even better, there have been a couple sightings of his wife along the same route, which raises our confidence level that it's actually him."

"How's that?" The president looked preoccupied. Like she was thinking of something else.

"It's the only place we're getting independent sightings of both of them," the director explained. "Not like the reported sightings of her in Alabama and him in Wisconsin."

He clasped his hands together. "When we're getting separate sightings of both of them in the same area, it's highly likely that they are actually there."

"And all your people are clustered in Nevada," Alana pointed out, not bothering to mask her frustration at his failure to capture the Nelsons when they were right under the FBI agents' noses.

"My people are everywhere." He cocked his head. "The FBI has a resident agency in Medford. That's in southern Oregon."

"I know where Medford is!" Alana snapped.

She didn't really, but this guy had a way of getting under her skin. He was constantly talking down to her or wearing expressions that indicated he thought she was a moron.

"Well, then you know that Medford is most likely where they're headed, if they left Winnemucca and drove northwest to Oregon, as the sightings indicate."

"Of course." Alana's gaze swung to the president, who was looking at her fingernails, then back to the director. "I'll be looking forward to your next update. Perhaps you'll have nailed down their actual location by then."

CHAPTER THIRTY-FOUR

The other customers were shopping in the candy aisle, and the clerk barely looked at Katie as he rang up her total and handed her some change. Zach must have been praying, and God was surely listening.

She hurried back out to the truck and gave her husband a thumb's up. Moments later, they were back on the road. Headed for a store where she would once again appear without sunglasses or any disguise beyond a hat – which was no disguise at all. Maybe she could try to stuff all her hair up under her hat. At least then, it wouldn't look exactly the same as all the images of her now floating around the internet.

Soon, they pulled in to a big box store. The parking lot was jam-packed.

Katie tucked her hair into her hat, then stopped by Zach's window before she went inside.

"You might want to get a bunch of non-perishables," he said. "Looks like everyone else is getting ready for the apocalypse."

It was true. Shoppers were coming out of the store with carts piled high. And not just televisions and big stuffed animals, either. They had cases of water and food.

"I'll see how it goes." Apprehension laced her words. "I don't want to be in there too long."

"That's fine. Listen to your spirit."

She sucked in a deep breath and blew it out. "Okay. Here goes nothing."

Katie squared her shoulders and started for the entrance. The place really was a madhouse. Shoppers poured into and out of the building, jostling each other as they went.

And not a single one was carrying just one or two bags.

There were only three carts left in the cart return area. She grabbed one and rejoined the flood of humanity streaming into the building.

On the bright side, there were so many people, and they were so intent on grabbing everything, that they'd hardly notice her.

Then again, with so many people, the odds that one of them *would* recognize her went up astronomically. She kept her chin down and headed for the health and beauty section.

Hardly anyone was buying hair spray tonight.

In a few moments, she'd selected four boxes of hair color and dropped them in her cart.

Now, the big decision: hurry to the checkout and get out of here, or join the crazy horde and try to get more groceries?

She didn't need any at the moment, but it wouldn't hurt to have more staples to stretch out the camping food in the motorhome.

It was probably worth making the effort.

She lowered the brim of her hat and entered the crush of humanity headed for the grocery aisles. On the way there, she passed the electronics section.

What about burner telephones?

She would be paying with cash, obviously – so there shouldn't be any way to connect them to her and Zach. Snatching two off the rack, she dropped them in her cart, along with four data/minutes refill cards.

The grocery section was even worse than she expected.

Long sections of shelves were stripped almost bare. It looked like the photos of Florida grocery stores when a hurricane was coming ashore.

The bread aisle was wiped out. Only two cases of water remained, and those were seized by arguing men as Katie looked on. Good thing the motorhome had a big water tank, and it was full.

Grim-faced shoppers pushed carts with whatever they could find and afford. The canned soup section was nearly decimated, but Katie got three cans of chicken noodle soup. All the pasta was gone, but she got two big bags of brown rice and one bag of black beans.

Someone's cart smashed into her hip, pushing her into the old lady beside her.

The guy didn't even apologize.

Katie turned to the older woman. "Are you alright?"

The woman looked at her with wide eyes, and nodded. Then her expression changed.

"Say, aren't you that lady –"

"Nope." Katie grabbed her cart and backed away, then swung it around.

Time to get out of here!

Okay, that was a dumb move. She'd probably totally confirmed that woman's suspicions. Ugh! But there was nothing to do about it now.

She wove her way to the front of the store through a maze of shoppers and carts, finally reaching the self-checkout area. Signs on orange paper hung on each checkout, stating, "CASH ONLY." Two harried employees were on hand to manage problems and supervise all eight checkouts in their section. Seven were in use, so she pushed her cart to the remaining available station.

Katie wondered how much theft was going on tonight. Probably a lot!

She kept her head down and tried not to look at the camera that was recording her as she scanned each item. This store was nice enough to display the camera's video feed on a screen right in front of her face.

Lovely.

Did it have a facial recognition program? Were security guys calling the police right now?

She grabbed the bag of black beans and scanned it, but it didn't beep. Tried again. Nope. A third time, but the reader just couldn't scan in the UPC code.

Great. Now what?

Should she summon one of the employees? That would mean personally interacting with someone who might recognize her.

Should she leave the beans behind? She wasn't going to steal anything.

Seconds were ticking by. She didn't have time for this.

Sending up a quick prayer, she slid the bag one more time over the scanner.

It beeped! Hooray.

She dropped it into a bag with the rice, and quickly scanned all the hair dye, cell phones, refill cards and soup, then fed enough cash into the machine to pay for it all.

The lights flickered.

What?

The electronic readout looked like it was re-setting. Moments later, it appeared that it had "forgotten" her purchase, without spitting out a receipt... or her change!

"Do you have a license for that thing?" Evan asked, wondering about the gun in Elizabeth's purse. "Did you take a class or something?"

She didn't look at him when she answered. "Something like that."

He realized he might be making a fool of himself, but he was so intrigued he couldn't help it. Before he could ask another question, though, she glanced his way.

"You're bleeding." Her voice held no emotion. "There's a first aid kit on the floor behind my seat. You can turn on your map light and clean your cuts."

"I'm sorry. I hope I didn't stain your upholstery or anything." It hadn't even occurred to him when he got into her nice car. He'd been so worked up about the fight. Now, though, his palms and his knees stung.

"Don't worry about it," she said.

He reached behind the driver's seat and found the kit. She turned on his map light as he opened it. This was a serious trauma kit, not just a bandages and aspirin kit.

She carried a gun in her purse, and this in her car? Why?

He looked at her.

"Elizabeth... what did you say you do for a living?"

A long silence.

"I didn't say."

He waited. Until he couldn't stand it anymore.

"And you're not going to?"

Her Audi was so close to the back of his pickup that a tow strap between them would've been loose. He cringed, but kept his mouth shut while he waited for an answer.

"Can we talk about something else?"

"Okay. If you promise not to run into my truck!"

She touched her brakes, and Evan took a deep breath. But Elizabeth spoke first.

"Thanks for helping me back there. At the gas station."

As if he had forgotten.

"I'm sorry I wasn't there quicker. As soon as I saw what was happening –"

"No. Don't apologize." Her face turned briefly toward him. "I wasn't paying attention to my surroundings. It was so stupid!"

She was blaming herself because she was attacked? That was wrong.

"It's not your fault," he said. "Those kinds of scum are always looking for people to prey on."

"Which is why I should have seen them coming!" She slapped her open palm on the steering wheel. "But I'd just gotten a text from Dad, and –"

"Wait, you heard from your dad? What'd he say? Anything about Zach?"

No, of course it wasn't about Zach. That was just Evan's wishful thinking. He stared at Elizabeth's darkened face.

"He's in D.C. Got my message that I'm headed to Canada with your family, and said to get there as quick as we can. He'll try to join us later." She glanced his way. "Nothing about Zach, sorry."

Alana joined a huddle with the president, CIA director, and director of Homeland Security.

"We believe the Iranians sent that bomb," the CIA chief said. "Even if one of the big terrorist organizations ends up taking credit for it, we have to believe they were sponsored or aided by Iran."

"Why?" Basilia crossed her arms. "Why couldn't it have been the Russians or North Koreans?"

"Because we found some communications over the past few days between Governor Abdullah's son and certain Iranians, specifically his uncle, who has terrorist connections. The governor's wife is Iranian, you know, and she has been visiting her brother in Iran, and she's still there."

He looked around furtively before continuing. "Of course, we know the governor's son was involved in the California attack, and we suspect his uncle in Iran may be the ringleader for the whole operation. The son was supposed to fly to Iran yesterday, but was caught in the fires after his helicopter crashed."

Alana closed her eyes for a long moment.

Oh, this was not good. Not good at all!

If this news broke – that the governor of California's Iranian brother-in-law was the instigator for the New York nuke – how long would it be before some intrepid reporter discovered that the governor's son had led the attack on California?

And Basilia's decision to frame Zachary Nelson might backfire.

On all of them.

She glanced at the president, whose wide, unblinking eyes looked haunted.

"Maybe we should rethink this thing about Zachary Nelson," Alana suggested.

"No!" Basilia swallowed. "I know what you're thinking, but we have to stay the course. We can't have Americans blaming the Muslim community for all this!"

"But –"

"I said, 'No!'" The president glared at her. "I've made up my mind."

Alana gave a single, silent nod. She wouldn't argue with the president, and it was clear she couldn't persuade her.

While she might have made a different choice, this decision was Basilia's to make, not hers. And if things went badly, Basilia would take the blame for it.

Meanwhile, Alana needed to give the president as much support today as she possibly could. Because she was tormented, and it showed all over her face.

CHAPTER THIRTY-FIVE

The checkout machine owed Katie more than $15, as well as her receipt for her purchases.

She'd have to call an associate over to help. Glancing around, she saw all the other self-checkout machines appeared to have the same problem. The momentary loss of power in the building had caused them all to blank out and reset.

Some shoppers were repeatedly swiping the touchscreens. Others were calling for the associates. Two had begun re-scanning their purchases.

It'd take a while to sort this all out and get help to get her change and her receipt.

That was time she didn't have. Especially if whoever was monitoring the checkout security cameras had recognized her and called the police.

She could live without her change. It was time to go.

If anyone stopped her, the machine should have a record of her payment. Unless it was lost when the power flickered.

That was a risk she'd have to take.

Katie picked up her bags and started for the door, trying to look nonchalant instead of suspicious. She kept her chin up, her shoulders down, and avoided eye contact with anyone.

A moment after she passed through the first set of doors into the entryway, an alarm went off.

What?

She forced herself to continue walking.

All her items had been scanned – and paid for.

People started staring. At each other, at her, at the guy behind her... she glanced back at him.

A twenty-something pudgy white guy with a bad case of acne, he was pushing a cart with a flat-screen TV. That thing might have set off the security alarms.

He didn't slow down.

Katie hurried to stay ahead of him, exiting the second set of doors at a brisk walk. Behind her, the wheels of his cart rumbled faster and faster.

He was making a run for it!

She stepped to the left, getting out of his way before he ran over her.

A quick look back revealed two uniformed security guards running through the first set of doors.

She glanced toward the motorhome and kept walking. The guards blazed past her at a sprint, then the acne guy abandoned his cart and kept running. The cart smashed full speed into a shiny black Chevy Tahoe beneath a parking light.

Katie winced. That'd leave a dent.

She hurried to the pickup and got in, glancing toward the RV. Zach's form was barely visible in the darkened cab. She gave him a thumb's up, and got one back in return.

Soon, she was steering the pickup toward the exit, glad to be away from this place. And glad to have made her purchases.

Now, if they could just find somewhere safe and quiet to camp for the night.

They continued along the highway, driving past an airport

with no flight traffic, and soon approached I-5. Zach signaled his turn onto the onramp heading north.

The interstate was not very crowded, and they made good time. Within a few minutes, they were headed out of town. Lights from homes and businesses grew farther apart, and soon they were out in the country again, cruising along at a good pace, headed north toward Washington.

A half-moon illuminated the hills, and a blanket of stars twinkled in the sky.

Katie took a long, relaxed breath.

It was good to be out of town!

As they drove north along the dark interstate, Evan cleaned his hands and knee, then applied a topical antibiotic and some bandages to keep seepage in and dirt out.

"Sorry about the mess," he said, gathering the torn paper wrappers.

"Don't worry about it." She sounded preoccupied. "Okay if we listen to some music?"

"Sure." Maybe it would fill in the awkward gaps in the conversation.

She fiddled with the radio and settled on a classical station.

Another puzzle. What twenty-something woman listened to classical music? And then he remembered something from his childhood.

"Your mom was a musician, wasn't she?"

"A concert violinist." Her voice was low and proud. "First chair."

That explained the music selection.

"Do you play?" He asked. "An instrument, I mean?"

"Piano." She lowered the radio volume as the music rose into a crescendo. "And drums."

He grinned, glad the car was dark so she wouldn't easily see it.

Elizabeth. A gun-toting beauty queen drummer. A true conundrum, if he'd ever met one.

He tried to wipe off his grin with his hand, just as she looked his way.

"What?" A puzzled expression wrinkled her brow, illuminated by the taillights of his pickup, which she was far too close to again. *"What?"*

"You're a tail-gating, gun-toting pianist drummer!" He laughed. "I can't figure you out!"

She braked, extending the distance to his truck.

"And what are you?" she asked. "You haven't said anything about yourself. But you attacked that creep at the gas station like a ninja."

She glanced his way. "You studied martial arts, didn't you?"

"Guilty." He met her eyes. "Just for a year, in college. I'm pretty rusty."

"Where'd you go to college, anyway?"

"Georgetown," he said.

"You always were a brain. When we were kids."

"I was a geek when we were kids."

Truth was, he was still a geek. He just hoped she didn't think so.

As Dick Chalmers approached, Alana noticed something about him that reminded her of a hunter. Maybe it was the way he moved, or a certain look in his eye – she had a hard time nailing it down, but at the moment he was almost smirking. Hopefully that was a good sign.

"Great news!" The FBI director grinned as he stopped in front of her. "Zachary James Nelson has been located!"

He clasped his hands together in front of him and looked at her expectantly.

"Where?" Alana asked, trying to sound bored. They'd been through this almost-got-him excitement already. And lost the guy in Winnemucca.

"Medford," he said. "It's in southern Oregon."

As if she still didn't know where Medford was.

Alana's eyes shot directly to the ceiling. She dragged her gaze back down to his, and blinked. Then sighed.

"How do you know?"

There was no way she was going to give him the satisfaction of acting enthusiastic.

In no way was he getting her hopes up again!

"He just triggered the license plate readers." The director was still smiling like a Cheshire cat. "We've got agents on the ground there. We'll have him within minutes."

Maybe. But it wasn't the first time Alana had heard that today.

"He's on I-5, driving north," he added. "We'll set up roadblocks, use helicopter spotters –"

"I thought air traffic was grounded," she interrupted.

He looked at her like she was daft.

"Not for law enforcement and emergency responders." He glanced at the small conference room, where they'd met earlier with Ambassador Wilford. "I've got my team setting up some live feed in there. You can join us, if you want."

Of course she wanted to see that. But she didn't want to act too excited about it.

"Yeah, okay. I'll be there in a minute." She turned and made her way to the coffee table, never glancing back.

The last thing she needed was coffee. It was far, far too late for that.

She was still entertaining the notion that she'd get some sleep tonight. Caffeine would wreck all that. She chose herbal tea instead, then let her gaze meander around the PEOC, trying not to think about what was happening outside of Medford, Oregon. It didn't work.

She had to know.

Moments later, she was opening the door to the small conference room.

CHAPTER THIRTY-SIX

Tension seeped from Katie's muscles as the interstate wound through quiet hills sprinkled with farms and small communities. Somehow, the darkness made her feel more secure. It cloaked her family in obscurity and anonymity.

She yawned and rolled her shoulders.

Eventually, hopefully soon, she'd get to crawl into bed and collapse into sleep. She was more than ready. Zach must be getting tired, too.

This whole ordeal had been exhausting.

She couldn't wait to have it behind them. Or just lay low in the forest, waiting for it all to blow over once the feds discovered their error in blaming Zach.

There was no way she could continue on like this tomorrow, driving and dodging the public and police. Nope. Things had been bad enough today.

No way was she going anywhere tomorrow. She might not even get out of the RV.

Zach was really making good time. He rarely drove above the speed limit in the motorhome, but tonight he was going at least five over.

She tried not worry about it.

Did he know where he was going? Had he found something on the map that looked good, while she'd been in the store?

She certainly hoped so. Another hour like this, and she'd be falling asleep at the wheel.

About twenty minutes after they left Medford, she started seeing more lights ahead. Must be approaching another town.

Great. More people and cops.

Well, at least they'd be able to cruise through under cover of darkness.

Suddenly, Zach signaled a turn off the interstate.

Why here?

She followed him off the highway, and they drove over a bridge. Dark water flowed beneath her as she read the sign: "Rogue River."

It sounded like a place they might like to explore – when life was normal. Now, it just felt foreboding.

They followed a curvy, narrow highway that hugged the black bends of the river as it rushed west, toward the ocean.

Katie kept expecting a deer to leap out of the thick brush along the highway and crash into her pickup. Across the river, headlights from traffic on I-5 illuminated the freeway.

Emergency vehicles flashing red and blue lights screamed up the interstate, and she was glad to be on this side of the Rogue, winding slowly toward the Pacific.

Were they looking for Zach?

She doubted it. They were probably going to an accident scene or something.

Besides, how could they have tracked them here, to southern Oregon? They hadn't used their credit cards, and they'd ditched their cell phones.

There was that warning that Evan had texted, about staying off the interstates. And they had, most of the day.

Well, they were off the freeway now.

But they were approaching another town.

And that made Katie groan. She couldn't wait to be far, far away from populations of people and police.

A helicopter flew up the river, spotlighting the ground below. Then I-5 curved slightly north, and the chopper and the emergency vehicles faded in the distance.

While the new town loomed up ahead.

Katie followed Zach through quiet neighborhoods, then their little highway approached larger, intersecting highways. They'd have to make a decision here. Left or right, north or south?

The sound of a helicopter throbbed overhead, and its spotlight illuminated the highways ahead.

The chopper circled, and the light circled with it, lighting up each vehicle on the roads below. In a moment, that would include Katie's and Zach's.

In the distance, a siren pierced the night air.

This town was bizarrely busy with law enforcement activity.

Slowly, the reality of the situation sank in... somehow, they'd tracked Zach here. And now, they were going to trap him.

At Erie, Elizabeth followed Evan's parents onto Interstate 90, traveling northeast toward Buffalo, NY. Evan couldn't suppress a yawn. What a long, crazy day it'd been!

Now it was late and he was tired, and suspected Elizabeth was, as well. She'd finally stopped tailgating the pickup about an hour ago, though.

"If you get tired of driving, we can trade off," he suggested.

She glanced his way. "No, I'm good. Plus, we're getting close now."

Close was a relative term, but yeah, if all went well, they should be in Canada within two hours. As the night wore on,

Evan had become increasingly convinced the leaving the U.S. was a really good idea.

He wished he'd done it yesterday, when Zach first suggested they head out to Galloway. Then he and his parents would have been safely ensconced in Canada before New York got bombed and all the financial weirdness began.

On the other hand, if they'd done that, Elizabeth wouldn't be with them now. So this was definitely better, by far.

He yawned again and leaned back in his seat. Last night, he hadn't slept much, knowing his brother was trying to get away from the fires.

And today Zach was trying to get away from the feds. But he was smart, and Katie was smart, so maybe they'd be okay. Plus, they were praying people. If God could save them from the fires, maybe he could save them from the feds, too.

Otherwise, they were toast. Evan couldn't imagine how they'd be able to evade the authorities otherwise, given all the technology and tracking and surveillance the government could deploy.

Evan's eyes were tired. He decided to let them close.

Just for a minute.

The tension in the small conference room electrified Alana as she stepped inside. FBI agents had set up monitoring equipment with audio and video feeds from the Oregon agents on the ground and the helicopters in the air.

She took the only open seat, which was next to Director Chalmers.

He ignored her, leaning forward to study the video on the largest screen.

Alana returned the favor, saying nothing to him.

Muffled helicopter rotors thumped quietly in the background

as video showed footage of intersecting highways. Spotlights illuminated dark vehicles on the roads, then moved to nearby streets and circled back again.

"You don't think they'll notice this activity and avoid it?" Alana hated to ask, but couldn't help herself.

"We've got roadblocks up everywhere." He didn't glance away from the video feed. "If we don't catch them at one of these intersections, we'll catch them on one of the roadblocks."

Finally he glanced at her. "There's no place they can hide."

"We'll see." She folded her arms and leaned back in her chair.

Her nonchalance didn't make a dent in the excitement in the room. And honestly, she felt the thrill of the hunt, too.

She just didn't want anyone else to realize it. Particularly not Dick Chalmers.

As the seconds ticked by, though, it felt like her pulse synched with the thumping of the helicopters. Her back straightened. She leaned forward, tensed like a cougar about to pounce on its prey.

Zachary James Nelson was down there, in one of those vehicles.

She could feel it. Almost smell it.

Her eyes fixed on the screen.

In a minute or two, he'd be in their clutches.

CHAPTER THIRTY-SEVEN

Katie clenched the steering wheel. The spotlight from a helicopter flooded the road just ahead of Zach. When it circled over the intersecting highways, Katie saw a second helicopter.

This one lower. Closer.

Any moment now, the RV and the pickup would be illuminated by their spotlights.

Her heart thumped.

Her eyes searched left and right in the darkness, but she couldn't see any escape. A prayer, like a thought, flashed through her mind.

Zach's brake lights came on, and Katie slammed on hers to avoid running into him.

Her breath caught in her lungs.

Suddenly, Zach was turning left, across traffic.

She couldn't see where he was going, but she followed him. Then her headlights illuminated a dark alley, bouncing off old brick walls colored with wild graffiti.

Moments later, he steered into another sharp left.

Now they were on a side street, going the opposite direction of their previous travel.

Away from the highways.

A helicopter roared over the side street, thundering louder than Katie's heart. Its light blazed over the RV, then over the pickup.

She held her breath.

Were they recognized?

Maybe not yet. The big bird continued on to join the two already circling the highway intersection.

Zach swung a right at the next street, and Katie barely had time to make the turn. Thankfully, there wasn't too much traffic tonight.

She thought they were traveling south now. The street took them through a residential area, with multiple developments leading off from both sides of the main road. Illuminated upscale homes dotted the hills, and cookie-cutter ones lined the lower streets.

Did this road go anywhere?

Would they be able to get out of here without turning around?

That'd be a trick with the motorhome. It didn't do U-turns very well.

A siren blared through the night.

It sounded close.

Less than two blocks ahead, Katie saw what appeared to be a main street.

Zach's brake lights came on as he pulled over to the curb. Katie stopped behind him. She killed her lights, and he did a moment later.

Up at the intersection with the main street, a police cruiser drove into view, lights flashing. Katie's heart hammered.

Would he turn onto their street?

Had the police somehow tracked Zach's exact location? Had that helicopter team spotted them and called them in?

Evan woke with a start. Where? What?

He looked around. Right... he was in Elizabeth's car. And she was exiting the freeway, following his parents in the pickup. The off ramp was packed with vehicles, even though it was the middle of the night.

"Was I out long?" Before she could answer, he asked another question. "Where are we?"

"We're in Buffalo," she said. "You napped a while. And snored."

Oh, she had to be joking! He rubbed his eyes.

"How bad was I?"

"Awful." She looked his way and grinned. "No, I'm just kidding. You didn't snore at all. But you drooled!"

He wiped at the corners of his mouth. It was dry. "Really?"

She burst into laughter.

"No, not really!"

Not far ahead, he saw signs for the Peace Bridge border crossing. And traffic was crazy! Everybody and their cousin was fleeing the United States. Especially New York.

The bridge had three lanes, and the center one had been reversed to accommodate two lanes of travel into Canada. Vehicles crammed those two lanes full. The one coming into the U.S. was nearly empty.

"Oh!" Elizabeth whirled toward him. "Do you have your passport?"

He felt his pockets, even as he realized the answer.

"No. It's in the console in the pickup!" His cell phone was in his pocket, though, and he pulled it out. "I'll call Dad."

"Phones aren't working," she reminded him. "What are we going to do if they go through customs ahead of us, with your passport?"

Evan looked up. Dad and Mom were only two cars ahead of them in line, and the line was moving about ten miles per hour.

"As soon as we get close to the customs station, we'll slow down. I'll get out and run up there," he said.

He tried the phone just in case.

And had no luck, as Elizabeth predicted. Maybe it was from damaged towers here in New York, maybe it was from the solar storm, maybe it was from too many people attempting to use too few connections.

In any case, cell phones had become totally unreliable. At least in the U.S.

Alana's pulse quickened. There was something about hunting someone down, something exhilarating, something she'd never experienced before.

It was a battle of wits with another human being, in which the other person was in mortal danger, whether he knew it or not.

Did Zachary James Nelson know it?

Certainly he knew he was wanted, but did he know they wanted to kill him?

Alana inhaled suddenly. She'd been so mesmerized, she'd stopped breathing. Her lips were dry. She moistened them with her tongue.

Another breath, deeper this time. Her tense muscles were starving for oxygen.

She raised her shoulders toward her ears. Everything felt so taut.

Director Chalmers turned toward her.

"Pretty awesome, right?"

He watched her reaction. Didn't elaborate. Clearly, he sensed how she was feeling. He had to be feeling the same himself.

She nodded without speaking.

Didn't want to break the spell.

Something about all this was sick. And yet, that sickness was what was drawing her in... that dark, dangerous, twisted thing.

Murder.

While she'd never call it that aloud, she could admit it to herself.

After all, she'd set this whole thing up. With the suggestion of California's beloved governor, and the blessing of the president, of course, she'd framed this man.

And then suggested that he not be brought in alive.

Earlier today, the notion made her queasy.

But now, as it was finally happening, in the darkest night of America's history, it filled her with... what, exactly?

Excitement? Thrill? Bloodlust?

All of that, perhaps.

But there was something more.

It was power. In the darkest, truest sense of the word.

CHAPTER THIRTY-EIGHT

Katie froze as she watched the police cruiser enter the intersection ahead. Would he turn in here?

She and Zach were parked less than a block from him. Surely he'd see them!

But the street was dark, with few lights.

Maybe...

Maybe...

She sucked in a breath. He was going on past!

Zach didn't pull out after the police car was gone. He remained parked along the curb.

Was he okay?

Katie's thudding heart began to return to a normal pace.

Suddenly, a second cop car came into view in the intersection ahead – this one without lights or sirens.

They never would have known it was coming. If they'd pulled out after the first officer had gone by, the second one surely would have caught them!

How did Zach know to wait?

His lights came back on, and he began to pull back onto the street. Katie eased out behind him.

When they came to the intersection, Zach turned right.

What was he thinking?

They'd be following the cop cars!

Obviously he knew that, too, so hopefully he had a good reason for doing this.

Tension knotted her shoulders as she gripped the steering wheel, her eyes searching left and right, watching for trouble. Being behind the wide RV, she couldn't see everything ahead of her, but she kept checking her mirrors for police approaching from behind.

One set of headlights was back there, perhaps a little more than two blocks. There was no way to know if it was a cop, until it was illuminated by a street light.

It didn't really look like a police car, but it might be an undercover one.

Soon, Zach signaled a left turn on another main street. After Katie followed him through the intersection, she saw helicopters with spotlights in her rear view mirrors. They were searching along the highway back there.

Exactly where Katie and Zach would have been, if they hadn't suddenly taken this circuitous detour.

She was totally lost in a strange town, but at least she was moving away from the obvious danger. The motorhome took a right, and she followed it.

If she wasn't totally disoriented at this point, she'd say they were traveling west again. After a few minutes, and several more turns, they approached a small highway and turned left onto it.

Far behind her, the helicopters' spotlights flooded the highway intersection.

Flashing red and blue lights made it obvious those cop cars had set up a roadblock there, too.

This was the highway Zach had been aiming for all along!

If they'd proceeded as planned, they would certainly have been caught or stopped while attempting to get on the highway there.

Zach picked up speed, and Katie stayed close behind him. Soon, the helicopters and flashing lights disappeared behind them.

Katie breathed a sigh of relief and a grateful prayer.

Once again, they'd narrowly avoided capture.

Now, if they could just find a safe place to sleep for the night! Not that she was the least bit sleepy at the moment, but when this adrenaline wore off, she was going to crash. Hard.

As they made their way across the Peace Bridge toward the Canadian customs station, Evan watched the dark waters of the Niagara River flow into Lake Erie.

At the same time, he watched and waited for the traffic queued in the customs lines to slow down. Obviously Canada was still letting U.S. citizens into their country, which was a great thing, and one he didn't expect to continue for very long – but he needed a chance to run up to the pickup to retrieve his passport.

Once they were fully on the Canadian side of the bridge, traffic slowed, and his lane came to a stop.

"I'm going for it!" He released his seat belt, jumped out, and sprinted up to the truck.

The look on Mom's face when he rapped on her window made him think she was going to have a heart attack. Quickly, she rolled down the window.

"What are you doing?! You about scared me to death!"

"I need my passport! It's in the console," he said.

Dad turned on the interior lights, opened the console and started looking.

"It should be right on top. I put it there when we left Galloway, so it'd be handy when we got here." Evan watched traffic begin to creep forward again.

"I don't see it," Dad said. "Your sure it's in the console? Maybe you put it in one of the door pockets, or the glove box?"

"I'm positive!" His chest tightened. He had to have that document to enter Canada!

Dad rummaged around some more. "You sure have a bunch of junk in here."

"Let me look." Mom started fishing around in his stuff.

Evan's pulse throbbed in his ears. It had to be there. Where else could it possibly be?

"Found it!" She pulled it out triumphantly, then handed it to him.

By now, Dad was holding up traffic. But he didn't start driving.

"Elizabeth has a handgun," he said. "She can't take it into Canada."

Evan looked around. They were on Canadian soil.

"We're in Canada already!"

A horn sounded, then a second.

"She'll have to figure out what to do," Dad said. "They won't let her in, and I think it's a felony up here."

Another horn blared.

"Gotta go." Mom began rolling up her window. "Good luck!"

Something wasn't going right. Alana couldn't put her finger on it, but she sensed a shift in the force of energy.

As she watched the video feeds, everything looked good. At the roadblocks, each vehicle was stopped and examined. More helicopters had joined the search. Not just intersections now, but all nearby streets and every highway.

Still... something didn't feel right.

Beside her, Director Chalmers squirmed in his chair. He sensed it, too. She knew he did.

He had to, he was a hunter.

It was as if the balance of power had shifted.

A few minutes ago, she'd sensed more power than she'd ever felt. The power of a god.

A living, breathing goddess.

With the power to take life, if not give it.

But now, she felt energy draining away from her, like the ocean pulling back its tide. She couldn't hold onto it. It was going out, dragging the power with it.

"This is taking too long." Dick Chalmers shuffled his feet under the table.

"You lost him." Alana placed the blame right where it belonged.

"Not necessarily."

She hoped he was right. Perhaps she was being impatient. But he said it himself. It was taking too long. They should have had Zachary Nelson by now.

She willed herself to sit quietly and keep watching the video feed.

They might still find him. Maybe she'd spot him, and be able to point him out.

As images of roadblocks and vehicle searches filled the screens in front of her, she pressed her fingers to her lips.

Eventually, she'd have to tell the president.

They'd lost this guy.

Again.

She hated the thought of having to do that. Basilia was clearly becoming overwhelmed with all of the devastation and destruction this weekend had wrought on the country.

Would she be able to bear more bad news?

Because bad news was all Alana had to give her. They weren't catching this guy tonight. She could feel it in her bones.

She could sit and watch these screens until dawn broke on the west coast, but she wouldn't see Zachary James Nelson.

He was gone.

CHAPTER THIRTY-NINE

Katie followed Zach west along the Redwood Highway. City lights faded, and were replaced by smaller lights illuminating farm homes and barnyards. The road wound through little communities called Wilderville and Wonder.

Then the lights became fewer and farther between. Mountains rose up on both sides of the curvy, two-lane highway.

She yawned, then blinked. Fatigue was drawing her irresistibly deep into its clutches. Her body grew weary and her eyelids heavy.

Zach must be exhausted, too. They really had to stop, and soon, before they fell asleep at the wheel.

She was just about to radio him, when his blinker came on, signaling a right-hand turn onto a Forest Service road.

Oh, thank the Lord!

It wouldn't be long before they could fall into bed. She couldn't wait to climb the rickety ladder to the loft bed above the motorhome's cab.

The road ascended into the mountains. Curves and switchbacks cut along the forested slopes, leading up, up, up.

Katie's heart rose with it.

With every bend in the road, they were leaving civilization – and government – farther behind them.

Dust billowed from the tires of the motorhome, and Katie eased farther behind in an effort to let some of it settle before she reached it.

Finally, Zach flashed his brake lights twice, and then turned on his blinker. He must have found a place that looked suitable for tonight.

The motorhome pulled into a huge, flat, cleared area beside the road. Maybe it had been a landing for a past logging operation. In any case, there was lots of room.

Katie pulled in behind him, killing her engine and her lights.

She slid from the driver's seat, closed the door quietly, and walked toward the motorhome.

The interior and exterior lights blazed to life. The door flew open and Zach stepped out, with Duke at his heels.

Both bounded toward her. Zach caught her up in a hug that lifted her off her feet. He held her tight.

"We made it," he breathed into her hair.

"Just barely," she agreed. "Thank God!"

He set her down and kissed her. Duke nuzzled her hand and pressed against her leg.

"Let's put the little man to bed, and get some sleep." Zach took her hand and led her toward the motorhome.

"Amen to that!" Katie couldn't think of anything she wanted more.

Tomorrow would be a new day. They'd deal with it when it got here. For now, she craved the bliss of deep, restful sleep. And that's exactly what she'd have.

Evan jogged back to Elizabeth's sedan and climbed in, then reached for his seat belt.

"Got it?" she asked.

He held up his passport. "Yeah, but we've got a bigger problem now. Your handgun. Can we turn around, go back across the bridge to get rid of it, and come back?"

She reached instinctively for her purse, then looked around her, then fixed her eyes on him.

"I can't get out of this line!"

Evan cussed. He ran both hands through his hair. Then turned to her.

"Okay, here's what we'll do – just pretend like it's not there. Be cool. They probably won't check your purse."

She shook her head. "That won't work. They always ask about firearms."

"So lie!"

"I can't." She stared ahead, where Evan's parents were just reaching the inspection station.

"Are you kidding? Of course you can. And you better!"

Even in the dim light, he saw her face blanch. Her fingers tightened on the steering wheel. She looked left and right, like a scared rabbit.

"Elizabeth!"

She looked his way. The whites of her eyes were massive.

"You can't tell them about it. They'll take you to jail. And probably me, too!" Evan hissed. "Then we'll be deported back to the U.S."

She moistened her lips.

Mom and Dad cleared customs, and the car ahead of Elizabeth moved forward. She eased up behind it.

Pulling her purse onto her lap, she opened it.

"What are you doing?" he asked.

"Getting my passport!" She retrieved it, handed it to him, then zipped the purse closed and put it on the floor behind his seat. "Do you pray?"

"I wish I did," he said.

"Well, you better start right now!"

The vehicle ahead of them pulled forward, and Elizabeth waited for her signal to approach the guard's window.

"I'm not sure how," he said.

"Beg for help!" She eased the Audi up to the window.

If only it was that easy! Evan panicked. He tried to calm his breathing and look normal. He hoped Elizabeth would lie.

He didn't want to go to jail. Or back to the United States as it collapsed this week. He wanted to join his parents in Canada.

Closing his eyes for just a moment, he followed Elizabeth's advice and begged. Please, God, if you're real, get us out of this mess! Let us get through!

A female border officer greeted Elizabeth, who took both passports from Evan and handed them to her. She flipped them open to their photos, then peered through Elizabeth's window at Evan. He hoped he hadn't developed a black eye from the attack at the gas station.

Elizabeth sounded perfectly calm as she answered questions about where they were traveling, how long they planned to stay in Canada, and whether they had any fresh produce in the vehicle.

Another border officer approached the first woman and interrupted her, then whispered something to her.

Evan's heart thumped. What was this about?

Abruptly, the first officer turned to Elizabeth and handed back the passports.

"Welcome to Canada," she said hurriedly. "Enjoy your stay."

"Thank you," Elizabeth said.

Before she shifted into gear, the two border agents got into a heated discussion.

"What do you mean, 'closing the border?'" The lady asked.

The guy held up his hands. "Don't ask me! That's what they said. We have to start shutting this crossing down!"

Elizabeth pulled forward, surging into Canada.

Evan expelled a shaky breath. They'd made it! Just barely, apparently.

But they were nearly out of cash. And who knew how long their credit cards would work up here? No retailer in their right mind would accept plastic from U.S. banks, once they understood the devastation that had been unleashed on the American financial system.

Alana steeled herself to face the president. How she hated being the bearer of bad news! But she'd stayed in this little conference room watching the FBI search in Oregon for over an hour, and they hadn't caught the guy.

Obviously he'd seen the road blocks or helicopters, and managed to scurry down some little side street like a rat hiding in an alley.

If he hadn't already found a way to sneak out of town, maybe they'd find him tomorrow.

But the president would want an update tonight.

Alana pulled herself out of her chair and left the room, saying nothing to Director Chalmers or his team. She was sure her expression said everything.

Theirs did, as well. Defeat was written across every face.

The PEOC was quiet as she entered. A lot of staff had left. Including her own.

And Basilia wasn't in the room.

Alana approached the president's chief of staff.

"Is the president taking a break?" she asked.

Grace Denver looked up from the computer she was powering down. "She's out for the night. She left nearly an hour ago."

"Oh." Alana glanced at the clock on the far wall. Almost 2 a.m. "Thank you."

She hadn't realized it was so late.

Morning would be here soon, and sleeping in wouldn't be an option. If she wanted to get any rest at all, she needed to head to bed now.

She started for the door, dreading a bout of insomnia. Knowing she'd have to deliver bad news in the morning, sleep would not come easily to her.

On the other hand, perhaps it was fortunate that the president had already retired for the night. At least now, Alana didn't have to give her the bad news right away.

Basilia had already been on the edge of despair. More frustrating disappointment might send her right over the cliff.

And who knew? Maybe they'd catch the guy in the next few hours, and she could give Basilia good news in the morning.

THE END.

But if you wish to continue this series,
look for "America"
and "Oregon."

ACKNOWLEDGMENTS

Readers and friends – Thank you for reading, and for your support. God bless you.

Special thanks to John Rock and Deb Motley for their feedback, prayers and encouragement.

Candle Sutton – My excellent critique partner, dear friend and partner in prayer. Heartfelt thanks!

My husband – You are the best. Thank you for your support of this project, and all my other crazy ideas.

Jesus Christ – My life and breath, my inspiration and the giver of all good gifts. Thank You.